LAWLESS &
TILLEY

Lethal Harvest

MALCOLM ROSE

SCHOLASTIC

For Juliet, Ross, Ben and Sam

Scholastic Children's Books
Commonwealth House, 1–19 New Oxford Street,
London WC1A 1NU, UK
a division of Scholastic Ltd
London ~ New York ~ Toronto ~ Sydney ~ Auckland
Mexico City ~ New Delhi ~ Hong Kong

First published in the UK by Scholastic Ltd, 1999

Copyright © Malcolm Rose, 1999

ISBN 0 590 63731 2

Typeset by TW Typesetting, Midsomer Norton, Somerset
Printed by Cox & Wyman Ltd, Reading, Berks.

10 9 8 7 6 5 4 3 2 1

The only sounds were the quiet hum of the pumps and the bubbles breaking gently at the surface of the water. At the bottom of one of the tanks, a sea anemone had trapped a fish with its milky-white poisonous tentacles. The small fish, paralysed but still alive, was being sucked slowly into the anemone's stomach where digestive juices had already begun to dissolve its flesh. Soon, only its skeleton would remain. In the next aquarium, a speckled sea hare slithered over a large round stone and disappeared behind it. Although a vegetarian, the grotesque sea hare had a toxin that could kill small animals. In another tank, three blood-red sea urchins sat in the crevices of a rock. Their long needle-sharp spines, loaded with venom, were waiting for the unwary.

The warmth of the water was carefully maintained

but the pale blue light made the room feel cold and uncanny. With its forty tanks of assorted marine life, occasional gurgling sounds and fishy smell, it was a place where nothing was left to chance. Temperature, saltiness, oxygen content and levels of lighting were all tightly controlled. Everything in the bio-prospecting laboratory was arranged for the comfort of its invaluable occupants.

Dressed in a spotless white overall, Dr Lipner's shoulders looked big and powerful like a swimmer's. He reached into the second aquarium, took the hidden sea hare expertly in his gloved right fist and dropped it into a beaker of pure alcohol. The marine organism writhed in the toxic liquid for a few seconds, then it lay still. The creature was dirty green with dark blue spots. It had the characteristic flaps of skin that looked like the ears of a hare, and yellow swellings over its slug-like body. Once, the Greeks believed that it had satanic powers. Now, it was a sad sacrifice to the advancement of humans. Science believed that it had pharmaceutical powers. Dr Lipner removed it from the intoxicating liquid with tweezers, placed it on a tissue and dabbed away the alcohol. Placing the stunned creature on a balance, he noted its weight. Then he placed it on a white teflon tile. Just as he was about to pick up the scalpel, the laboratory door opened.

A man in a chic suit and flashy tie had a bundle of papers rolled up in his hand like a baton. He waved it at Dr Lipner and said, "Good report." When he stepped forward into the lab, a shadow fell across his face. "The shareholders will love it! According to this, we could eliminate skin cancer with Corstatin."

The head of Bio-prospecting, almost standing to attention before his managing director, replied, "It's got a dramatic effect on blood vessels. It shuts them down so they can't supply oxygen and nutrients to the tumour cells. The tumours wither and die. Just like that. And it's got no significant side-effects. But there *are* some problems. Corstatin's too complicated to make synthetically. We need large numbers of the sea slug to make it for us but they refuse to breed in captivity."

On the wall, an electronic clock showed the time and a date of Monday 4th August.

"Oh well, never mind, we'll sell it as a *natural* cure," the smug MD declared. "Always goes down well with the caring punters. I can see the advertising spin right now. Forget nasty men in white coats. Forget smelly labs. We go back to nature for a cancer cure: the green cure." He beamed with pleasure at a huge medical advance. And with the expectation of huge profits in a billion-pound-a-year market.

Jason Lipner picked up a small glass vial containing a light brown powder and held it out towards his boss.

"Is that it?" The lights made the whites of the director's eyes seem vaguely blue.

Jason nodded. "Ten *Dendronotus* sea slugs after they've been dried and ground up. We'll get a few

3

micrograms of Corstatin out of that – if we're lucky."

"Oh well," the director repeated.

"And this species of sea slug isn't exactly abundant," the section leader informed him.

"It's not exactly beautiful or high–profile either, so the environmental lobby won't kick up much of a fuss, especially when it can eliminate a cancer. Saving tens of thousands of human lives a year versus a slimy sea slug. That's not much of a contest."

In an expensive laboratory in Sheffield, a long way from the home of the sea slug off the coast of a tiny Caribbean island, it was easy for the MD to ignore the damaging effect of their company's needs on a tropical reef.

Dr Lipner divided his working time equally between South Yorkshire and Tobago. He did understand the West Indian issues but his loyalty to Xenox Pharmaceuticals was not in doubt. He announced, "One conservationist in Tobago *is* kicking up a fuss: a marine biologist called Dr Ellis McBurnie."

For a moment the MD's self-satisfied smile disappeared. "Well, get him off our backs, then. Lots of human lives depend on this. He can't stand in the way of progress. Get yourself back on a plane and put him out of the equation – any way you can. Do you hear me?"

Dr Lipner nodded. "I'll get on to it."

The MD turned and hurried away from the lab. Jason picked up the scalpel and set about dissecting the luckless sea hare.

It was only when Ellis was swimming with the fish that he felt truly alive. He fitted the snorkel's plastic mouthpiece between his teeth and, with relish, descended the steps at the side of his launch into the warm, shallow Caribbean Sea. As a marine biologist employed by the University of West Indies, Ellis was permitted to enter the Buccoo Reef marine park where the tourists were not allowed to go. It was reserved for conservation and scientific study. Ellis was on his own with just the reef life for company. Exactly how he liked it. The water was perfectly clear and the reef was only a metre or so below him. In places it had grown upwards so much that it nearly reached the surface of the sea and he could not swim over it. The colourful coral looked delicate but Ellis knew that, if he scraped against it, it would cut his skin like rough and unforgiving concrete. Really, the coral was sharp, rugged and vicious. But, in another way, it was fragile. Wherever a human being came into contact with it, growth ceased. The coral died. That was why tourists and their boats had been banned from the area. Slowly, visitors would damage and ultimately destroy the beauty that attracted them to the site. That was why Ellis hoped that the reserve would be extended and the tourist area restricted even more.

With the relentless afternoon sunshine on his back, Ellis swam lazily over grey coral that looked like discarded human brains, some bloated to enormous size. He peered down on pillar coral like the fingers of two huge hands protruding from the sea-bed as if a giant had been buried upright and his dying action was to thrust his hands up out of the sand and into the water, praying for mercy. Brown branching corals and pale green sea fans littered the reef, giving it the appearance of a leafy forest.

While he snorkelled, Ellis was at one with nature. The fish allowed him into their idyllic domain. Some even swam with him, welcoming him to their fantastic world. Below him, a chunky male parrotfish glided, looking as if someone had thrown yellow paint into its face. It was turquoise with yellow streaks on its head and gill covers. The yellow blotches had also spattered on to several of its fins. Curious about Ellis, the fish swam beneath him for a while, mirroring his every move. A fully grown trumpetfish, seventy centimetres in length with its unmistakable and hugely elongated mouth, hovered, head down and ghostly still, among large branching corals. Trumpetfish came in a variety of colours but this one was bluish grey with several rows of iridescent green spots down the length of its narrow body. As soon as it saw Ellis it turned away unhurriedly and uninterestedly. Ellis's favourite, a queen triggerfish, swam in front of him as if leading him to a secret place in the reef. The fish, usually called "old wife" in Tobago, was spectacular. Green upper half and yellow lower half, splashed with shimmering blue. Ten wispy black lines radiated from the fish's eye like a childish drawing of eyelashes. A poster or photograph, no matter how colourful, could never do it justice.

To Ellis's trained eye, the reef was much more than exotic fish and coral. He saw charm even in the crawling nudibranchs, or sea slugs. They deserved the name because, in shape and mobility, nudibranchs were like slow and slimy land slugs. Yet the marine versions were not so drab. Many were dressed in extravagant colours as a warning that they oozed foul or even poisonous chemicals as a defence against predatory fish.

For a while, Ellis trod water to watch a *Dendronotus* writhing in slow-motion across a coral, seeking a tasty anemone. The sea slug was not very attractive or graceful, Ellis had to admit, but it had its place in the ecology of the reef. It was an orange and brown bag of chemicals, covered in outgrowths that looked like miniature cauliflowers. The finger-shaped extensions in the folds of skin that covered its head and mouth gave it a perverse fringe of dreadlocks. To Ellis's disgust, a British pharmaceutical company was interested in the lowly *Dendronotus* because of its poison. Perhaps it would make a good medicine, a chemical weapon for attacking cancer cells in humans. But what would happen to the creatures if the chemical company harvested them? The delicate balance of reef life would be upset. Perhaps drastically. Perhaps fatally.

So far the chemists had plundered only a few of the sea slugs for their tests but now that its poison had proved to be valuable they'd be back to capture many more. And the Tobago Government would let them. It would sell the permit to the company at some incredibly high price. The income from the trade would be good for the island. After all, it was only one ugly species of sea slug. Yet when the Buccoo habitat had been stripped of its *Dendronotus*, the drug company would move on to other Caribbean reefs and harvest those as well. In the rush for profits, the natural population of *Dendronotus* would be wiped out. The repercussions for the reef were unknown. If the pharmaceutical chemists ever learned how to breed the creature in tanks, it would be reduced to a factory-farm existence in the service of humanity. And only one lone marine biologist was prepared to make waves on behalf of the nudibranchs. Ellis had come to regard himself as defender of *Dendronotus*. Lost in thought, he kicked his legs and continued his swim.

At the edge of the reef there was a sheer drop. Really, the reef was growing on the top of an enormous cliff. Rather than looking down into the blackness of the abyss, Ellis turned to swim back across the reef, taking a different course. But before he'd moved away from the brink, he experienced a sudden sharp sting in his left leg. He was puzzled and shocked. He knew of no species that would sting like that. He had not stood on a sea urchin, a camouflaged scorpionfish, or a barbed shell. A coral graze was not so sharp and he was nowhere near a white-tipped fire coral. It wasn't the bite of a moray eel. Besides, morays had become rare in this part of the reef since another pharmaceutical company had culled over eight hundred kilogrammes of them to extract less than a thousandth of a gramme of a toxic substance for chemical study. And Ellis knew that he had not been stung by a jellyfish. That was like several pin pricks at once or the lash of a whip. Very different. No. Nothing stung like that. And there were no species in the Caribbean that were lethal to humans. Except one, of course. Other humans.

In the last hazy moments of consciousness, Ellis wheeled round and saw a scuba diver disappearing into the dark depths below him. He couldn't even tell if it was a man, woman, boy or girl but the figure was weaving back out to sea.

Contact with a human being was killing Ellis as well as the reef.

3

On Monday 11th August, at the harrowing conclusion of their previous case, Detective Inspector Brett Lawless and Detective Sergeant Clare Tilley were asked to assist the inquiry into the death of a marine biologist and conservationist who lived and worked in Tobago. The request to South Yorkshire Police wasn't a random choice. The Tobago police force was concerned that Xenox Pharmaceuticals in Sheffield might be involved in Ellis McBurnie's death. McBurnie had been poisoned and a drug company would know all about poisons. He had clashed with Xenox because he'd claimed that the company was endangering a sea slug for a microscopic amount of a "miracle" cure for human skin cancer. He'd made a stand against Xenox's exploitation of his beloved marine environment. And the choice of Brett Lawless wasn't random either. The detective had studied bio-chemistry at university before joining the police force, so he possessed the necessary expertise.

Brett and Clare flew out to the small Caribbean island on Wednesday 13th August with mixed feelings. They had wrapped up their last investigation with a great deal of credit but without a colleague, lost in the line of duty. In the eyes of the law they had succeeded, but they felt as if they'd failed. Even the tabloid press had poured scorn on their dogged pursuit of justice. Now they welcomed the break but Clare also dreaded the assignment. As a fair-skinned red-head, she knew that she would suffer in the tropical sunshine. She burned very easily. Ironically, she was a prime candidate for skin cancer.

Brett stretched out his legs and said, "Pity it's the height of the British tourist season and standard class was full, isn't it? It's tragic having to travel in first class luxury."

Clare smiled faintly and asked the flight attendant for another free gin and tonic. She glanced at her partner's concerned expression and said, "Well, the beer's rubbish and I've got to drink something."

Brett nodded. "I know. I'm just not sure it's the best way to get over the death of a friend."

"You do it your way, I'll do it mine." Clare turned and gazed out of the small window of the jumbo jet. Somewhere below her there were miles and miles of the Atlantic ocean but all that she could see was unending cloud like a giant snowy plateau.

Begrudgingly, Brett glanced through the Caribbean case notes again. Ellis McBurnie had been a part-time employee of the University of West Indies on Trinidad, but he had been based on Tobago. A respected biologist, he had been, in his spare time, a tourist guide to the reef. Even from the brief notes, it was obvious that he had been wedded to the island and its marine wildlife. He had studied it and, at the same time, had wanted to show it off to visitors, yet keep it unspoiled. A difficult balancing act. He had written a book about life on the reef and it sold well to visitors in souvenir shops and suppliers of diving equipment. Ellis was thirty-three when he died, married to Umilta McBurnie, also an experienced diver, and he had no children. His body had been found, washed up on a beach, by a tourist taking a moonlight dip at midnight on Thursday 7th August. Brett put down the report and sighed. It was just a coincidence, he knew, but it provoked an unsavoury memory. Because Tobago was five hours behind Britain, Ellis's body had turned up at exactly the same time that Brett and Clare were conducting the fateful raid on Oughtibridge: five o'clock last Friday morning.

In an attempt to distract his partner for a while, Brett held up the folder and asked, "What do you think? Smell anything?" He wasn't being funny. He had come to realize that, even without concrete evidence, Clare had a real instinct for finding crooks – a police officer's nose. He was learning to appreciate it even if her feelings couldn't be exhibited in court like a smoking gun.

She shrugged. "I could close my eyes and stick a pin in it, if you like."

"Maybe after you've spoken to a few of the suspects."

"Maybe," she replied. "But it smacks of one of your cases. Chemistry, biology, drugs, a university scientist and tropical fish. You'll love it."

With a grin, he said, "But I'll miss the traffic jams, the derelict steel works, the hustle and bustle, the burglaries…"

The plane landed first in Trinidad, Tobago's bigger neighbour. Once the tourists bound for Trinidad had left the jumbo, a large number of locals took their places. They boarded the plane rowdily, carrying shopping bags and shouting cheerfully to each other, as if it were a bus. They seemed to be returning to Tobago after a morning spending-spree in Port-of-Spain. One jumbo-sized woman got on with a loud laugh and a hot jumbo-sized pizza. The smell wafted appetizingly down the aisle.

As soon as everyone was seated, the plane taxied away from the terminal and made the short hop to Tobago. From the now cloudless sky, Tobago looked beautiful. Long and narrow with a convoluted yellow outline. The shape of a sea slug nestling in a blue ocean. There was the protruding green canopy of the rain forest at its back end and the airport runway at the creature's mouth. The aeroplane began its descent before it had reached any great height. The woman's pizza was probably still hot when the passengers filed across the baked concrete towards passport control.

"Wow!" Clare murmured. "The heat." She put her hand across her brow to shield her eyes from the sun.

"Hope you packed your shades," Brett said with a broad smile.

They were expected in the terminal building. The tourists in the queue were treated to a rum punch while they waited, but Brett and Clare were whisked through Customs quickly with just a glance at their passports and police warrant cards. Speed was unnecessary, though. Allen Rienzi, their contact in the local force, had not yet arrived.

When he turned up, fifteen minutes later, he shrugged. "I guessed your flight'd be delayed in Trinidad. It usually is. Still, it's nice here. No problem waiting. Everywhere's nice here. No hurry." He was in his mid-thirties, well built, only slightly overweight, and nearly as tall as Clare. He was dressed in grey shorts and a bright yellow short-sleeved shirt. His shiny sunglasses stopped Brett and Clare seeing into his eyes. His brow glistened with traces of perspiration. "I was taking a crab dumpling at Miss Jean's when I heard the plane. Miss Jean'd be insulted if I didn't finish it off before leaving." His voice was deep, with a tinge of carefree humour. Or was it a trace of cynicism about his guests? "Come on," he said. "I'll take you to your hotel. It's a fifteen-minute stroll."

Following Allen, Clare began, "Er… What about our bags?" She glanced back at the airport building.

Allen shrugged. "Relax. Don't worry about it, man. Enjoy the walk. The porters'll find out you're at Tropikist. They'll send your bags on – when someone gets round to it. We don't lose things here but they happen at our pace – not yours. We don't charge around in this heat. You'll get used to it."

The tarmac road, bounded by empty and scorched fields, had more pot-holes than cars. Brett and Clare had to slow their natural walking pace so that they didn't outstrip their new companion who strolled at the speed of Big John Macfarlane – without the excuse of massive weight. Near a large hotel, Allen shouted a greeting to a man selling exotic fruit from a parked van. Then he added, "All right for tonight at Turtle Beach?"

"No worries," the fruit vendor called in reply.

Further on, outside the building, Allen told his English counterparts, "That's a nice hotel. Crown Point. It's not yours, though. I couldn't get you into it."

Beyond it, Brett and Clare saw the sea for the first time since landing. It was a gorgeous turquoise. Some large birds were plunging like bombs into the water, submerging for a few seconds and then reappearing.

"What are they?" Brett asked.

"Brown pelicans – going fishing," Allen answered. Suddenly he stopped. "If you're interested in wild-life, it's right under your feet." There wasn't a pavement at the side of the road, just a grass verge and then an open gutter. "Watch," Allen said. Gently he put a foot on the green grass. Amazingly, the grass reacted to his touch. Its leaves curled up and showed their brown underside. It looked like instantaneous withering. He lifted his foot and did the same to another clump. In its turn, it curled up, turning from dark green to brown. "Even the grass is clever in Tobago. It plays dead when it feels pressure. That way, the animals don't eat it."

"How long does it stay like that?" asked Brett.

"A couple of minutes or so, then it unfolds." He nodded towards the ditch and continued, "At night these gutters'll be full of frogs, making sweet romantic music, singing to their mates." He took a deep breath of the clean air and gazed out to sea. Clearly he was proud of his island home, even if he was a little offhand when showing it to his visitors. He looked back at Brett and Clare and said, "You're younger than I expected for cops who come so highly recommended. But let's get something clear straight-away. I didn't call you in. I don't need you Brits on this case. We're not some backward British depen-dency, you know. We're not helpless without your big city crime tactics. No need for cavalry. I can crack it on my own, in my own way."

"I'm sure you could," Clare replied, annoyed that

the assignment she'd been given had hurt this man's pride. "So, who asked for our help?"

"My boss. He yielded to pressure from on high. The Government's Tourist Department doesn't like it when a dead body washes up on one of our best beaches in front of the holiday-makers. It spoils the scenery and puts them off. No tourism, no money. Apparently, they're only reassured by bringing in fancy cops from England."

"Well, since we're here we might as well give you a hand," said Brett with a smile. "Can't do any harm. We'll try not to get in the way."

"You can crash out on the beaches all day long and enjoy a few drinks. Have a nice time. You haven't got beaches like ours – and sun like this – in England. I'll tell my boss you're on the job."

"Very tempting," Clare replied, "but…" She pointed to her shoulders. "If these see a bit of sun, they go pink and start to peel."

Allen snorted. "You're a fine one to send! White and a red-head." He shook his head in apparent despair.

"Anyway," Brett said, "I understood we only got called in because there could be a Sheffield connection. Xenox Pharmaceuticals. Nothing to do with your ability to sort it out on your own."

Allen nodded. "That's the excuse my chief latched on to – to make me feel good about it. It didn't work." Hands on his hips, he looked down and then said, "The grass has started sunbathing again. See?

The first lot's back to normal and the second's coming out now."

Sure enough, the brown fronds were peeling apart, revealing the true colour of the grass again.

Allen led the detectives on, declaring, "Anyway, I've said my piece. We know where we stand now."

There was a field on their right where five black cows with impressive horns were chained. Beyond it, there was a long white two-storey building with balconies. "Tropikist," Allen said. "August is the low point of our tourist season. It's quiet. No carnival. At the turn of the year, after the hurricane season, we're knee-deep in Americans, so right now hotels take the chance to decorate and repair, ready for the onslaught. That knocks out a lot of rooms. The rest are occupied by European tourists but the staff found you a family room: one they're doing up. It's not quite finished yet so they couldn't put holiday-makers in it but I took a look at it. It's OK for you."

"A family room?" Brett queried.

"Uh-huh. I hope you guys get on well." Allen laughed aloud.

Telling them he'd be back in a couple of hours, Allen left them so that they could get lunch and settle in. Their second-floor suite consisted of one large living room with a double bed, kitchen area and a large revolving fan in the ceiling, a bathroom and a con-necting room with two single beds. The walls were only half painted, the wardrobe and some of the cupboards lacked doors. In the corner of the room, the air conditioning unit was humming noisily and dripped water every few seconds. The spilled water ran under a patio door and evaporated from the hot concrete before it got to the edge of the balcony.

The balcony overlooked the hotel's lawn, trees that drooped in the heat like willows, the play area, tennis court and, at the far end, a swimming pool, bar and dining area. Two young men were painting the tarmac of the tennis court. They weren't exactly rushing. In fact, they were sitting, relishing a cool drink and admiring the token area that they'd painted earlier. Beyond all that was the sea. No traffic noise, no clouds, no buildings, no pollution. Just lawn, beach, palms and perfectly blue sea. A haven. It was difficult to imagine anyone raising the energy to kill in such a serene place.

Standing outside on the balcony, Clare said, "It's … er … different from Sheffield."

"Just a touch," Brett responded, stretching his back after the seven hours in an aeroplane seat. "Impressive." A small yellow and black bird landed on the rail and hopped along it, watching Brett and Clare, probably expecting a titbit. When it realized that they had nothing to offer, it flew away. Brett put out his hand and felt the waxy leaf of a tree that was growing close to the building on the right of the balcony. "Well," he said, turning back towards the room. "What do you want: double or single bed?"

Strolling round the hotel and its grounds, Brett used his credit card to get some local currency: Trinidad and Tobago dollars. Tropikist was not a plush, expensive hotel but it suited Brett and Clare. There wasn't an indoor restaurant, only the covered outdoor area with white plastic tables and chairs at one end of the swimming pool. All of the other guests were Europeans. The family in the pool were shouting to each other in German. There were two English groups and one French at the bar. A small wooden jetty extended into the sea from the hotel premises. Brett and Clare walked along it and, while they tucked into club sandwiches, watched the orange fish swimming underneath them in the clear water.

"They look like goldfish," Clare commented.

"Blackbar soldierfish, actually," Brett told her, using his knowledge of tropical marine life. "I think so anyway."

Clare smiled. "You're in your element here, aren't you? Tropical fish."

"You will be as well," he said with a grin. "I sneaked a look at the menu. They seem to barbecue most of them. Barracuda, red snapper, grouper, flying fish. The lot."

"Sounds good. If I survive the sun, I'll enjoy the food," Clare replied. "By the way, while you're here being unfaithful to your fish back home, who's looking after them?"

Brett knelt down and dipped his hand into the sea while he answered. "I got a mate to go in each day, feed the fish, check the mail, bin the junk. That sort of thing." He looked up and said, "The water's really warm. Have you brought your swimming stuff? We deserve *some* relaxation."

Their suitcases turned up an hour later and Allen Rienzi returned after three hours. This time he had a battered old car and he offered to take them to Buccoo Bay.

"What's there?" Brett asked.

"A great beach, very popular with tourists. It's got coconuts, Vicky's café and bar. And a body – till we took it away. I just thought you'd like to see the beach and see what you're missing if you join this case."

Until they found their feet on the island, they agreed to Allen's ideas. Besides, they didn't want to test his patience further by rejecting his suggestion. They donned sunglasses and went with him.

The sandy beach fell away steeply where the Caribbean Sea slapped down on to it with gusto. Several children were playing in the breakers, which were large enough to be scary but too small to be seriously dangerous. It was quite blustery but the wind was warm. The lofty palm trees lined up along the edge of the curved beach leaned and swayed rhythmically. Allen pointed out to sea. "Fifteen minutes by boat – about two miles out. That's where he died. His body was washed up here." He spread out his hands towards a spot where two young couples were splashing in the waves.

"How do you know where he died?" Brett enquired.

Allen cackled. "No problem. Anyone round here knows the currents. And his deserted boat at anchor was a pretty big clue."

"Of course," Brett murmured. "What's out there?"

"Buccoo Reef, man. McBurnie was at the Marine Reserve, though not the part the visitors are allowed to go to and ruin."

"Any other boats out that way at the time?"

"Not very close," Allen replied. "Fat Maurice was on the tourist run. He was around the other end of the reef, No Man's Land or the Nylon Pool."

"Fat Maurice?"

"A big lad. He works his boats out of Pigeon Point

or Store Bay – that's just by your hotel."

An immensely tall and slender man with a tray of bracelets, necklaces, beads and music CDs walked past and slapped hands with Allen. "How's it going, man?" Allen asked.

"So, so. Europeans don't splash money around like Americans." The beach trader had an odd way of talking out of the corner of his mouth. He looked at Clare and said, "You want a bracelet, lady? I could do you braids but your hair's a bit short. That's a pity because I never done ginger before."

Clare shook her head. "Maybe some other time."

"It's a deal. See you again." He began to trudge further along the shore.

"If this Fat Maurice does trips to the reef," Brett continued, "doesn't that make him a business rival to Ellis McBurnie? Ellis ran trips to the reef as well."

Allen was surprised that Brett had taken in so much information about the case. And he was impressed by Brett's perception. "He sure did. I've spoken to Maurice, though. Maybe tourists don't spend so much at this time of year but there's still plenty of business for two. No problem. And word gets around it's a beautiful trip. Ellis and Fat Maurice could've doubled their charge and they'd still get takers." Allen paused before adding, "You should go on the tour, man. It'd do you good. Take a dip. They say the Nylon Pool has medicinal properties."

"Like the sea slugs," Brett muttered. "Anyway,

you're right. I'd love to see the reef. Only ever seen one in pictures before." He thought that both he and Clare could use medicinal properties right now to cure their wounded consciences. He was thinking that he'd also like to see Fat Maurice.

"Look," Clare put in, "I'm going to take cover under the palms. OK?"

While they walked to the edge of the beach so that Clare could stand in the shade, Allen said to her, "You want a hat, man, to keep the sun off your neck and face. You can get one at the shop inside Crown Point Hotel. My friend Janelle runs it. I'll make sure she gives you a good deal. You'll need it on the trip and the beaches."

"Thanks for the advice," she said.

"Talking of sea slugs and the reef," Brett said, "who've Xenox got here at the moment?"

"A small research team based in Scarborough. A couple of locals, one from Trinidad, two Americans. And they're led by Jason Lipner. He's white, from your place – Sheffield, UK – but he spends quite a bit of time here. Till the investigation's done, I've confiscated their passports. No idea what they do, these science types, but most of them think of this posting as a holiday. They don't exactly strain themselves."

"And?"

"And they've all got alibis."

"Good alibis?" Brett queried.

Allen shrugged. "Not foolproof. But don't worry

about it. Just get your hat, a cold beer, a spot on the beach and you're away. No problem."

Brett did not succumb so easily. "How did he die? What was the poison?"

Allen shrugged. "You need to speak to the pathologist."

The most active pastime on the beach was a make-shift game of cricket. The local lads had driven six sticks into the sand as the two wickets and, despite the fact that the sandy pitch sloped sideways, played remarkably well. Most of their energy went into bowling and batting. Runs between wickets were incidental and taken at a lazy rate, if at all. One set of stumps had just been demolished by a wickedly un-playable delivery and several cries of "Howzat!" shattered the peace and quiet.

"Where's the pathologist?" Brett enquired.

"Hold on, hold on," Allen boomed. "It's your first day. You guys aren't even acquainted with the island yet. The pathologist can wait till tomorrow. It'll mean a trip to Scarborough Hospital. Now, you relax. Enjoy."

"No hurry," Brett quipped, mimicking one of Allen Rienzi's many catch-phrases – most to do with unwinding.

"You got it, man. Learn fast but act slow." He beamed and then added, "Sluggish!" He laughed so loud that the whole island shook.

"His wife, Umilta?" Brett asked, unwilling to let go of his train of thought.

Allen waved his hands in the air and blew on them as if they were hot. "She'd light up any beach party. Know what I mean?"

Brett nodded. "But how did she get on with her husband?"

"I just told you."

"You did?"

"Ellis, he's into fish and sea slugs. Umilta, she's into music, enjoying herself." Allen wiggled his hips with surprising agility and rhythm. "Dancing."

"And diving. An experienced diver, the notes you sent said."

Allen grinned. "Look up and down this beach. You see maybe fifteen locals, including me. You see fifteen experienced divers. Like people in London are all experienced at going underground, we all go underwater."

"OK," Brett said. "But she *is* a suspect."

With a serious face, Allen spouted some home-spun philosophy. "If a man doesn't take an interest in a beautiful woman, she'll find an interest in something else. That's the way of the world." He looked first at Brett and then pointedly at Clare.

"Where was she at the time of the murder?" Clare asked.

"With a man she doesn't want to name."

Clare enquired, "Have you pushed her on that?"

"I don't need to," Allen replied. "I believe her. A neglected wife is going to get her … fun elsewhere."

Clare wanted to question Umilta herself because it

was plain that Allen wasn't going to open up and reveal anything else. Instead Clare remarked, "A two-mile swim's not impossible but it's pretty demanding. Are you assuming the culprit had a boat?"

"Round here, we swim better than we drive but, yeah, it's a job for a boat, this."

"Any evidence for someone being on Ellis's boat?" Clare asked. "Maybe someone got a lift out there with him, did the business and swam back."

Allen answered, "The trouble is, plenty of people have been in his boat. Mostly tourists. But there was nothing to suggest anyone was with him at the time. And, when he went to the reserve, he always pre-ferred to go on his own."

"Is there such a thing as a register of all boat owners on the island?" Brett queried.

"For sure. I've already got it, but it's not much use. I'll tell you, I've got a motorboat and all my mates use it as well. We're laid back about that sort of thing. They're used for fishing, earning a bit on the side by taking holiday-makers to an isolated beach, just messing around. Only the tourists with their own fancy yachts are protective, though there's not many of them till the Americans arrive later in the year." He looked at his watch and said, "Hey, I got business. You stay here. No problem. I won't be long."

Clare looked at Brett and smiled. "I *am* feeling the travel. Jet lag, I guess. I could use a bit of sand, scenery and shade."

"Me too." Brett flopped on to the dry sand and

stretched out luxuriously.

"Back soon," Allen told them. Then he ambled away like a man whose business would wait for him.

Clare whispered to her partner, "Soon could be hours."

"No worries," Brett replied, Allen-style. "Relax."

Clare shuffled into a comfortable position, smiled and closed her eyes. "Enjoy," she purred. Without opening them, she added, "I reckon it's an act, you know. Allen's casual all right, but when he has to move, I bet he's up there with the best of them. Leading from the front."

Behind them, a bright green lizard was perched sideways on a rock at the edge of the sand. Staring at Clare with an outsize eye, it was as still as death except that it blinked occasionally. Its face was not quite cute, ugly or cheeky. It was a curious mixture of all three.

After a few minutes of rest, Brett lifted up his head and looked at his partner. "According to Allen, everyone in Tobago swims, dives, and can get a boat," he said. "But, you know, not everyone knows how to poison. That's the angle to follow."

Without opening her eyes, Clare replied, "Once you get your teeth into something, you have trouble letting go, don't you?"

Brett laughed and admitted it. "It's wonderful here and yet ... I can't help thinking about Ellis McBurnie."

Among the breakers a couple of white kids

squealed with delight and alarm at a large wave that knocked them off their feet.

"Allen's not telling us everything, is he?" Brett continued.

"He knows more about Umilta and the poison," Clare replied, getting up on one elbow and squinting at Brett. "And he knows enough to doubt those Xenox alibis. Maybe he knows a lot more about a whole number of suspects he hasn't even mentioned yet. But put yourself in his position. It's a matter of self-esteem. He won't share everything with us because he wants to solve this crime. He'll probably dripfeed us information but keep some vital bits to himself." She paused before adding, "That's another angle. Butter up Allen to get more out of him. I can't blame him, though. We'd be the same if a couple of strangers threatened to take over a case of ours."

"True," Brett said in agreement. "I'd be as protective as a rich tourist with a fancy yacht."

Like unhurried holiday-makers, they both settled on the sand again.

When Allen returned, the afternoon was threatening to turn into evening. It was the time of day that Clare would come to appreciate the most. Peaceful, the smell of barbecuing food, warm but the sun too low to burn. Brett and Clare both realized that they had been dozing pleasantly.

"How do you want to eat?" Allen asked. "Local Creole, Indian, Chinese, European, anything else? It's all here, man. On Tobago, we're a weird mix. Race isn't an issue any more. We're Africans, Asians, Americans, Europeans all thrown together, all batting for the same team. So many influences. It makes for great food, great choice. Here, you'll get variety if you want it."

"How about a vegetarian who doesn't eat fish either?" Clare asked, jabbing a thumb towards Brett.

"Vegetarian!" Allen roared. "What's that? You can't survive on fruit and salad. You're a man, man. You gotta have fish, goat, chicken. You don't want to fade away!"

It was obvious that, if Allen had just been working on the case, he wasn't going to let on. He used food to keep the conversation from straying into an area that he regarded as private.

In the end, he took them to Miss Jean's at Store Bay, because it was a short walk away from their hotel and because Miss Jean concocted a few local vegetarian dishes. Her place wasn't a restaurant at all. It was a shack across the road from the bay and in the modest hut Miss Jean herself cooked and served. Near by, there were some rival stalls and a few shady picnic tables where people sat informally to eat and drink. Allen greeted almost all of them by name. He seemed to know everyone. Chickens strutted confidently around the area, clucking and pecking spilt food. They did not realize that one day they might be on the menu. A sleeping dog did not wake up, even when a chicken plucked a piece of bread from its bushy tail.

When Allen advised Clare to try the goat roti, she asked, "What is it?"

"Curried goat in a pancake. East Indian style. It's a local speciality. In Tobago, there's more goats than cars so you might as well eat them."

It wasn't a delicate meal. There were great lumps of cooked goat – including several substantial bones – in a large pancake.

"What do you think?" Allen enquired.

"Good, but... Tomorrow, I'll try the fish restaurant up the road. Smelled gorgeous."

As they ate, a huge red sun plunged rapidly into the Caribbean Sea on the horizon. Brett and Clare almost expected to hear the hissing of boiling sea-water. In Sheffield there were too many buildings and hills to get such an unobstructed view of sun-down. While darkness descended quickly, several people came up to Allen, slapping him on the hand or shoulder, and exchanged a few words with him. He had to be the most popular detective that Brett and Clare had ever encountered. They both wished that police officers in Sheffield could enjoy the same rapport.

Brett asked, "Who else have you got on your hit list – apart from Jason Lipner and his crowd, Umilta McBurnie and Fat Maurice?"

Allen shrugged. "Still muscling in?" He took the last bite of his own roti and then replied, "I've got my orders to co-operate with you, so I don't have a choice. I'll tell you. There's one awkward suspect: Haseley Abidh. I say he's awkward because he's a government minister. That makes him difficult to get to. He's in the Trade Department and he didn't like McBurnie's fiery brand of conservation one bit. It threatened a Xenox deal over the sea slug. And Abidh's eager to bring Xenox business – particularly their US dollars and English pounds – into Tobago to fill the island's coffers."

"But would a government minister get involved in murder?" Brett queried.

"He's a politician, man! He'll get involved in all sorts of things."

Brett said with a grin, "I'm glad to see your opinion of the profession is about the same as ours back home. Politicians must be the same all over the world. Is he on your list of boat owners?"

"Sure he is. He's got one plush motorized yacht."

"Have you spoken to him? What was he doing last Thursday?"

"Slippery customers, government ministers," Allen said, standing up abruptly. "But he wasn't at work that afternoon." He finished drinking a Coke from the bottle, put it down on the wooden table and announced, "I'm off. I've got an appointment at Turtle Beach Hotel soon. I need to get ready for it."

Now that Allen wasn't wearing sunglasses, Brett and Clare could see his eyes shining. He was looking forward to the appointment, whatever it was. "Anything we should be in on?" Brett enquired.

Allen bellowed once more. "I don't think so. I don't think it's you at all. Anyway, you know your way back, don't you? You can't miss it. And even if you do, you'll like where you end up."

"No problem," Clare retorted.

He was about to go but stopped and turned round. "Remember, up by the drains. Stand still and stay quiet for a couple of minutes. Then you'll hear it."

On the way back to the hotel, they took Allen's tip

and heard the magical sound of hundreds of frogs croaking in rhythmic unison. As soon as Brett or Clare took a step, giggled or said a word, the ghostly invisible choir ceased for a minute. Then, suddenly, it began again. Brett and Clare moved on when a lone car cruised past and silenced the chorus.

At Tropikist, Clare installed herself at the poolside bar with a Carib beer. She took a draught, pulled a face and muttered, "Pity they left out the flavour and the alcohol, but at least it's cold." With her forefinger, she played with the condensation that ran down the outside of the glass.

Intending to take a late-night swim in the pool, Brett asked her, "Coming in?"

Clare hesitated, clearly not in the mood for it. She looked down at her unfinished drink and said, "Perhaps tomorrow."

While Brett swam powerfully up and down the pool, Clare contemplated mournfully the risks of being a police officer, the toll it took on social life, the injuries she'd seen and sustained, the deaths she'd discovered and dissected. Lost in thought, Clare hardly noticed how many beers she was consuming. Then, on one of her visits to the bar, she spotted a stack of local newspapers that had been left, like magazines in a doctor's waiting room, for the benefit of hotel residents. She took a pile back to her seat and browsed through them. It would stop her brooding on the darker side of police work.

When he'd had enough of swimming, Brett stood

by Clare's table and dripped profusely. "That was great. Gentle exercise. You'd like it."

"While you've been enjoying yourself," Clare replied, "I've been hard at work."

Brett eyed the empty glasses on her table and said, "Really?"

She rustled the newspaper that she was skimming and said, "Really."

"Let's hear it, then."

"Try that." She pushed an old paper towards him and pointed at the headline, *More restrictions on reef visits?* The article explained that the coral reef was suffering from excessive tourist trips. In an attempt to reduce and contain the damage, the Tourism and Trade Departments were considering a further reduction in the area of the reef to which licensed tour guides were allowed to take visitors. There was a hint that the problem could also be solved by reducing the number of official guides from two to one.

Trying not to saturate the paper, Brett read the article and then checked its date. A week before Ellis McBurnie's death. Looking at Clare, he said, "You're thinking about a motive for Fat Maurice."

"Yes. And one of the people considering this cut-back on reef trips is Haseley Abidh. Tangled web, eh?"

"According to this story, the powers-that-be took statements from Fat Maurice – against a ban – and from Ellis McBurnie – for a ban – but their independent advice came from a coral reef expert, Lee Teshier. Local fisherman. I suppose the other two weren't to be trusted because of their vested interest in the tourist trade."

Clare nodded. "But look at this." She handed Monday's newspaper to Brett. She wasn't referring to the front page article on Ellis's death but a short piece buried on page five. The landing of an enormous blue marlin. For the benefit of the photographer, the fish had been suspended vertically by its tail from a crane with its sword-like nose nearly touching the ground. It was considerably larger than the proud smiling fisherman standing next to it, in front of a launch and a yacht.

"Wow," Brett breathed, looking closely at the picture. "That'd keep even you in barbecued fish for a day or two." Reading the report, he murmured to himself, "Record blue marlin catch by Lee Teshier." Brett glanced down at his partner and said, "He's described here as a fisherman and reef consultant for Xenox."

"Strange sort of independence, isn't it? An expert who's paid by slug-loving reef-stripping Xenox. Note the date of the catch as well."

"Landed on Thursday afternoon." Brett concluded, "Well, at least we know where Lee Teshier was at the time of the murder. Way out on the sea to catch a beast like that. Not your average inshore reef fish."

"Mmm." Clare raised a smile and said, "Perhaps

he's off the hook – unlike the fish. But still worth checking out."

"I must take it easy more often while you're working. It gets results." Brett spread his arms, rejoicing in the balmy night and beginning to relish the holiday atmosphere. "I can't get over this weather. It's late, I'm dripping wet, outside in my next-to-nothings, and I'm still warm. This is the life."

"I imagine the mosquitoes are enjoying it as well, having a feast on you."

"If I had a bit of alcohol in the blood, I'd pickle them."

Clare grinned. "All right, I'll get you one. What do you want?"

Clare claimed one of the single beds in the side-room and Brett occupied the double bed. Neither of them slept well though. Perhaps it was the heat, the noise of the air-conditioning unit, the unsettling feeling that they were still moving in an aeroplane, the unfamiliar total darkness, the smell of paint, the strange scratching and clicking of unseen wildlife. More likely it was thoughts of a lost colleague.

In the morning, they worked out a schedule that allowed them both their privacy and a fair share of the shower. Brett was at a loss. Normally in the early morning, he'd go for a run before breakfast. No one ran anywhere on Tobago – except between two wickets on the beach. It was too fiery to go any further. He guessed that exercise might be restricted to swimming in the evenings. He reached down and picked up his right shoe. Just before he slid his foot into it, a large black spider ran out and across his wrist. Brett shuddered involuntarily and shook the spider off immediately, dropping the soft shoe. The leggy creature scuttled across the floor while Brett cried, "Look!"

Moving surprisingly quickly, the spider dashed under the door and out of the room. Clare laughed. "You scared the poor thing."

"Poor thing? It could've been one of those vicious ones – incredibly poisonous."

More concerned, Clare asked, "Did it nip you?"

Brett looked at his wrist. "No."

"No problem, then. I still reckon it'd be more terrified of you than the other way round."

"Maybe." Brett seemed lost in thought.

Before breakfast, he went to reception and asked if anyone had been inside their room since they arrived. The receptionist told him that only the cleaner would go in and she wouldn't start till mid-morning. But Brett could not help thinking about the tree to the side of their room. Anyone athletic could have climbed up it, jumped on to the balcony and forced a way into the room.

Breakfast was a wide selection of fruit by the pool, followed by coffee that could revive the dead. Under her breath, Clare said, "You're wondering if someone planted that spider in your shoe deliberately."

Brett raised his eyebrows. "Well, there's at least one person who doesn't want us on the island."

"Allen? I know he organized the room and vetted it but…"

"I meant whoever killed Ellis McBurnie."

"Yeah. OK. But planting a spider's a funny way to scare us off. Or get rid of us."

"It'd be pretty daft in Sheffield, but here…" Brett shook his head. "I don't know. You may be right. Could be my active imagination. And maybe it wasn't poisonous. But, just in case, let's get this investigation wrapped up before something else turns up in our room." Then he brightened up and smiled. "I don't want anything to come between me and these open-air meals." Finding his enthusiasm for outdoor eating, he said, "Terrific."

Clare prodded several chunks of exotic fruit that she did not recognize. "Bet it's good for the digestion," she murmured sceptically.

On the ground and on vacated tables, several of the yellow-breasted birds – bananaquits – hopped around cheekily, searching out left-overs. A man with a large net walked slowly round the swimming pool, scooping up the dead insects that were floating on the water. Overhead, a plane came in low like a noisy mechanical bird of prey, bringing another batch of tourists.

Brett swallowed a small pill of Rifampicin, an antibiotic that he'd been prescribed for an infection he'd picked up from his tropical aquarium. Fish-tank granuloma dotted his right arm with a line of blue marks.

On the way back to their room Brett and Clare walked past the partially painted tennis court. The two lads were beginning a leisurely half-an-hour of painting before taking a break. After that, it would be too hot for work till late afternoon.

It wasn't long before Allen Rienzi arrived to drive the British officers into Scarborough, via Crown Point Hotel where he persuaded Clare to buy a wide-brimmed hat from his friend Janelle La Ronde. Clare probably paid a grossly inflated price but at least the hat would protect her face and neck from the scorching sunlight.

As they headed for the capital, Brett asked Allen, "Apart from you and your boss, who knows about me and Clare coming here, what we're here for and where we're staying?"

Not paying a great deal of attention to the road, Allen looked at Brett with a puzzled frown. "Not many. The hotel staff, the politicians in Trade and Tourism who decided you'd be a good idea, a few other police officers."

"Umilta McBurnie, anyone from Xenox, Fat Maurice?"

"Nope. Why?"

Casually, Brett dismissed it. "Nothing."

Their first appointment was with Allen's chief. A man totally unlike their own Detective Chief Superintendent John Macfarlane. He was slender and, like every islander Brett and Clare had met so far, dressed informally. He wore loose trousers and a thin flamboyant shirt with short sleeves. On his desk a whirring fan blew air, making the room seem fresher than it really was. The boss reminded Brett and Clare that, while they were police officers in England, in Tobago they were merely Allen's advisers. They had no more power than any other citizen or visitor. No power to search, charge or arrest. But they could question suspects, particularly the Xenox research team.

"We'd like to get a word with Haseley Abidh," Brett put in.

"Haseley Abidh," the chief repeated. He sighed and looked up at Allen. After his officer nodded at him, he said, "I'll see what I can do. I'll try and get you an appointment. Anyone else?"

Brett decided to be bold, to startle them. "Lee Teshier," he announced.

"Lee Teshier? Who's he?"

Trying to hide his surprise, Allen answered, "A fisherman. He collects samples from the reef for Xenox."

"That makes sense," the chief responded. "Allen can organize it. It doesn't need me." Standing up, he held out his hand first to Brett and then to Clare. "Despite the circumstances, I hope you enjoy your visit to our island. We're very fond of it. And we want it kept free of serious crime. You can help us do that." Addressing all of them, he added, "Tobago's not a place where murders should happen. You three have the job of sorting it out before we get any more."

Back in the car, Allen asked, "How did you know about Lee Teshier? He wasn't in the report."

Brett nodded at Clare. "Observant detective who checks through newspapers."

"Lee's got a cool alibi, you know. No problem."

It sounded to Clare as if Allen was acquainted with Lee Teshier but she didn't want to pursue it until she had talked to the fisherman. "I know," she interjected. "But he might have useful information."

"Where are we going next?" asked Brett.

"The hospital, in the east end of Scarborough, then Xenox headquarters. I've already asked my questions so I'm leaving the bowling to you. That's the best way of getting you into the game, like my boss wants. See if you can knock any bails off. Me, I think you should slow down a bit. All this rushing about's no good for the blood pressure. I can do without the stress, man. And it's no way to get to the truth. Truth takes time."

Brett smiled. Another homespun principle from Allen. Brett guessed that he had a vast store of them.

The pathologist didn't have to refer to her notes. She probably didn't tackle a sufficiently large number of deaths to forget individual details. "Ellis McBurnie. He drowned – sort of. Really he was too experienced a swimmer to drown, you know. He was killed by a poison while he was swimming. There was a tiny puncture wound in his left leg where it had been injected with something like a syringe. It was a fast-acting barbiturate that anaesthetized him almost immediately. He'd be confused, choke and then pass out. Paralysis would follow in a few seconds. While he was unconscious, he breathed in lots of seawater."

"When exactly?"

She checked the date on her watch. "Exactly a week ago. Thursday 7th August. About three o'clock in the afternoon."

"What poison was it?"

"Not something native to the reef," she admitted. "Thiopentone." She paused before adding, "It's a synthetic drug, you know, not native to anywhere."

Brett wondered what her facilities were like. Basic, he estimated. Perhaps she didn't have access to state-of-the-art analytical instruments. "Where was the toxicology done?" he enquired.

"We're not as primitive as you're thinking," she said with a wry smile. "We've got quite a few of the right techniques because we have to deal with tourists who come in after standing on all sorts of marine life that protect themselves with poison. And there's the locals who've overdosed on various folk remedies, you know. We get a lot of body fluids to analyse. In this case, though, to be sure, I sent samples to Trinidad as well. They went to the big hospital there and the specialists at the University of West Indies. They confirmed thiopentone."

"Where would someone get it round here?"

The pathologist grinned. "Right here – or in any other hospital, say, on Trinidad. It's a widely used anaesthetic, you know, not hard to come by."

"Do you know who markets it?" Brett asked.

When the pathologist shook her head, Brett turned to Allen Rienzi but he merely shrugged unhelpfully.

"The point is, do Xenox make or supply it?"

"I'll check," the pathologist said. She picked up a phone and dialled the pharmacy within the hospital.

While he waited for an answer, Brett asked Allen,

"Did you send out divers to look for a syringe or something similar on the sea-bed?"

"I led them myself," he replied. "Nothing. Maybe it wasn't ditched, or maybe it fell off the edge of the reef. The bottom currents could have pushed it anywhere."

The pathologist put the phone down and said, "They checked the stock for me. It's supplied by a US company, not Xenox."

"Thanks." Brett was thinking that it did not necessarily mean that Xenox did not have the anaesthetic. Just as aspirin could be bought from several different pharmaceutical sources, perhaps a number of companies sold or made thiopentone. Including Xenox. Besides, any of them could simply buy their own stocks of the barbiturate.

Allen drove back through Scarborough with his elbow poking out of the open window. His cotton shirt billowed in the breeze. The capital had none of the spacious elegance of the tourist centres. And it was nothing like its coastal counterpart in Yorkshire. It was a dusty ramshackle place, crowded with colourful concrete buildings lining narrow chaotic streets. Taxis and vans were parked everywhere, queuing everywhere, going nowhere in a hurry. People shouted banter across the street, drank outside cafés, shuffled down the streets laden with huge shopping bags. Allen leaned out of the window and called, "How goes it, Giselle?", "Up to no good again, eh, Sonny?" and "Wilton, how're you doing?"

Clare recognized Wilton as the tall chap who had offered her bracelets on the beach yesterday. She leaned close to Brett while Allen was talking to someone out of his window and whispered, "The man's Christmas card list must be endless." The driver behind simply waited for Allen to finish his conversation. He didn't even sound a horn impatiently. If Allen had been driving so erratically in Sheffield city centre he would have been lynched by now.

On the outskirts, the houses were mostly wooden with tin roofs. Many were painted in lurid colours and had dishevelled outbuildings made of old advertising hoardings. They were either storerooms or toilets.

To make sure that Clare would understand the nature of Xenox's business, Brett explained, "Pharmaceutical companies call it bio-prospecting. They take a ton of fish or whatever, mash them up and isolate a tiny amount of a substance that's active in humans – a potential new medicine. Really, it's just looking for biologically active substances – often poisons – or cottoning on to old wives' tales."

"Old spouses' tales, surely," Clare joked. "What do you mean, though?"

"Folk medicine, potions. If someone's great great granny says sliced fox lungs are good for asthma, or American Indians use the bark of the cinchona tree for treating malaria, scientists used to call it superstition. Not any more. They'll look into foxes' lungs or the cinchona tree to see if there's really active stuff

– a cure – in there. If there is, maybe they've got the next money-spinning drug. Like people used to prospect for gold in rivers, these people prospect for drugs in living organisms. Bio-prospecting. Some say using what nature provides is better than making new, unnatural substances in labs. Of course, it's not better if you're a fox, a cinchona tree, or a sea slug. Or an endangered species."

Eventually they arrived at a small laboratory overlooking Rocky Bay on the western edge of Tobago's capital. The Xenox outpost was nothing grand but it was much less cramped than the properties in the centre and far neater than the people's townhouses. Obviously, it benefited from foreign investment.

Inside, it wasn't luxurious but it was functional and had an air of quiet efficiency. The police officers were taken through a chemistry laboratory and then a windowless room containing about twenty large tanks teeming with aquarium life. Not just fish but snails, squirts, sea hares, worms and plants. The place purred with the sound of pumps aerating the tanks and motors circulating the water. There was no lighting in the room except for the twenty diffuse glows of the illuminated aquariums. The effect was spooky, like spectral radiance from watery graves.

Dr Lipner's office was small, crammed with books and journals on marine biology, medicines and health. On the remaining wall space there were posters, including a huge sea-bed map of the Buccoo

Reef area with detailed underwater contours. The desk was occupied by a computer and fax machine. Jason sat on one chair and waved the two English detectives towards the other two seats. Clare placed her new hat on her lap. Allen slouched against a filing cabinet.

"I'm not sure how we can help you," Jason Lipner stated bluntly. "We've already spoken to the police." He glanced at Allen Rienzi.

"No harm going over it again, man."

"I just wanted to get up to speed with some general information," Brett said. "I hardly need to tell you we've been brought in from South Yorkshire for the obvious reason. Location of Xenox headquarters. If there's been any … wrongdoing by your company, it might have to be pursued by South Yorkshire Police, not locally here."

Jason's gut reaction was to defend his paymasters. "Well, I can assure you…"

Brett was not interested in flat denials. He wanted information. He interrupted, saying, "I need you to tell me all about your potential cure for skin cancer. Not as profitable as a cure for AIDS, no doubt, but important?"

"Very," Dr Lipner stressed. "Skin cancer's the most common cancer in humans now – and rising faster than any other malignancy. The death rate's tripled in the last forty years, despite medical advances." By the look of Jason's shoulders, upper arms and chest, he probably worked out with weights. He was physically strong, no doubt. And he showed no sign of mental weakness. He was certainly not nervous or intimidated by the three detectives in his office.

"Wouldn't the best way of reducing skin cancer be to stop destroying the ozone layer – prevention – not to produce another drug that cures us once we've got the disease? And to work on early diagnosis – I thought it could be removed quite successfully if it's detected early enough."

"Absolutely," Jason agreed. "But Xenox is a pharmaceutical company. We can't plug the ozone hole and we can't make people go to their GPs when their moles start to grow, bleed or itch. A European branch of Xenox is working on better sun protection creams but we've also got to deal with the situation as we find it. The malignancy doesn't hang about once it appears and it's deadly when it spreads. That's the reality we have to deal with." Passionate about his work, he continued. "That's where we can make an impact – with a cure for advanced cases that escaped early detection. That's thousands of mortalities every year worldwide. A lot of people are going to be extremely grateful."

"Very worthy," Brett replied. "And it's bio-prospecting that's given you this breakthrough. Corstatin from a sea slug's going to revolutionize skin cancer treatment, you think. Do you know its chemical structure?"

"Of course," Jason answered. "But our chemists

haven't had any joy synthesizing it in the lab so far, so we're still reliant on harvesting the sea slug."

"Why not just take a few and breed them?"

"We're trying. Despite our best efforts, they fail to thrive in captivity. But the work continues."

"So, you'll need to harvest a lot of sea slugs. Possibly the lot." Brett's eyebrows rose questioningly.

"Obviously, it's not in our interest to make them extinct," Dr Lipner insisted. "Until we've learnt to keep and farm *Dendronotus* artificially, or until we've isolated the gene responsible for making Corstatin and implanted it into a more convenient organism that we *can* farm easily, or synthesized Corstatin in a lab, we depend on the sea slug. We wouldn't want to endanger it, would we? Besides, there are lots of other reefs that the slug inhabits."

"But if you strip the local one, you'll harvest the others as well?" Brett replied.

Jason sighed with impatience. "Before then, we're sure one of our ways of producing Corstatin will be successful. Most likely the farming idea."

"Poor old sea slugs," Brett muttered.

"Is that a silk shirt you've got on?" Jason pointed out. "There's no difference between breeding sea slugs for drugs and farming silk worms for their silk. Except silk's for vanity and Corstatin will save lives. As regrettable as it might be, we *do* need to harvest Buccoo Reef to keep us going, to help us bring farming or one of the other methods to fruition and save thousands of human lives."

Clare chipped in, "I'm in the highest risk category for skin cancer – white, easily sunburnt – so I'd go along with that. A cure's worth it."

"Exactly," Jason said, pleased to have a police officer on his side. "For the good of humanity, we're now waiting to see if the Tobago authorities are going to give us a permit to harvest the *Dendronotus*."

Brett asked, "Is there any doubt you'll get one? Tobago needs Xenox's money and the only voice raised in opposition has been … eliminated."

"Not by us," Lipner retorted. Then he added, "As for the permission, we don't know. We just wait in hope. We're quietly confident."

"What dealings did you have with Ellis McBurnie?" Brett enquired. "What clashes?"

"His point of view was different – opposite, as you said. But don't get me wrong, we respected his opinion. His was a valid standpoint and we didn't doubt his sincerity. But we did doubt his assessment of the threat to the reef and his priorities. No doubt, people dying of skin cancer – and their families – wouldn't appreciate Dr McBurnie's argument that the life of a sea slug should be put before a cure." Jason's eyes darted towards Clare because he imagined that she would agree with his outlook.

Firmly, Brett said, "That doesn't tell me what clashes you had with him. You personally or any of the staff here. Did you have face-to-face meetings? Did you offer him money to back down? Did he ever threaten you or the company? What went on?"

"We certainly didn't try to pay him off. That would've been useless. He was a man of principles, not after cash. But there were little ... incidents. Accusations and counter-accusations. Nothing initiated by us and nothing physical on our side. I'm sure the local police are well aware." Again, Jason glanced up at Allen.

Brett still wanted the story direct from Jason Lipner. "Give me some examples. Did it stay within the normal bounds of healthy debate or did it go further?"

"McBurnie had a go at our collector, Lee Teshier. He tried to talk him out of co-operating with us and tried to keep him away from the reef by blocking, maybe even ramming, with his own boat. Another time, Lee's boat was mysteriously holed. As you might expect, McBurnie also put pressure on the Government to turn the marine park into a conservation only area when it was put aside for both conservation *and* scientific study." Jason hesitated, thinking of other encounters. "I never met him in private but we had a couple of public debates on the use of the reef. Nothing was resolved – even though our arguments were far more persuasive. Shortly before his death, these premises were broken into. Tobago isn't like Sheffield, Inspector Lawless. Burglary's almost unheard of here. So, I think we can guess who was behind it. Anyway, he was disturbed by one of the staff coming to work late. Presumably Crawford scared him off before he could do whatever he came to do because nothing was damaged."

"Did your colleague – Crawford – actually see this intruder and identify him as Ellis McBurnie?"

"No."

Brett asked, "Did any of the staff here meet McBurnie socially or in private?"

"I wouldn't have thought so. No."

"We might need to come back and talk to them sometime," Brett said. "But, for now, where were you last Thursday afternoon?"

Jason Lipner grimaced. "I've been through this. I was seeing someone in Speyside."

Brett turned to Allen with a questioning look.

Allen took the opportunity to inject a jibe at his clueless competitor. "You need a tour of the island, man. Speyside's right at the other end, near the rainforest."

"Who did you see there?" Brett asked Lipner.

"An old woman. A Mrs Isabella McShine. Word got to me that she took a certain species of frog from the rainforest and used an extract from it on open wounds to help healing and stop infection. That could be interesting to a drug company." He smirked. "Why do you think we're on Tobago? There's a few locals into folk remedies and potions made from the wildlife. Herbs, spices, snakes, fish. There's plenty of inspiration for a pharmaceutical company here. Anyway, I offered Mrs McShine quite a bit but she was wily. She wouldn't tell me much – just enough to intrigue me. It's a type of market haggling. She expected me to go back afterwards with a doubled offer, no doubt."

While her partner asked the questions, Clare read one of Lipner's posters. It was a recipe for "divine water", apparently a genuine extract from the New London Dispensatory of 1678. *Take the whole carcass of a man violently killed, with its entrails, cut it in pieces, and mix them; distil it from a retort twice or thrice. It is reputed to have a magnetic power; if to one drachm of this water you put a few drops of the blood of a sick person, and set them on fire, and they mix, the sick recovers; if not, the sick dies.* Clare flinched at the ultimate in bio-prospecting.

Trying a different approach, Brett asked Jason, "Do you keep any barbiturates on this site?"

"Barbiturates?"

"Come on, Dr Lipner," Brett uttered. "It's a simple question. I don't have to explain what a barbiturate is to a pharmaceutical chemist."

"No, we don't," he answered. "Our work doesn't come close to them."

"And what about other branches of Xenox? If you needed some, could your parent company supply them?"

"I don't know where this is leading," Dr Lipner muttered. "You'll have to call Sheffield for that information."

"But you could order barbiturates from another pharmaceutical company, presumably. No questions asked."

Jason spread out his arms. "We're in chemistry. We can order what chemicals we need – within our budget."

"Have you ordered any barbiturate drugs?"

"No. One of my staff could show you the order books if you like."

Jason sounded so confident that Brett refused. "I don't think that'll be necessary. Perhaps I'll take a look if we come back to talk to the rest of the staff." But he didn't have any faith that an order for a chemical destined to be a murder weapon would appear on an official record of purchases. It would be a slapdash killer who was caught like that and this murder showed all the signs of careful planning and professional execution. Besides, Dr Lipner could have smuggled the drug in from England or another member of his international team could have sneaked it into Tobago among their personal baggage.

Before the detectives left the Xenox building, Lipner glared at Allen Rienzi and asked, "When will I get my passport back?"

Allen provided the answer that both Brett and Clare expected. He said, "Hey, what's the rush? Who wants to leave paradise?"

"When?" Jason repeated.

"When this case is put to bed," Allen replied. "Soon. Or whenever."

O ver a fruit cocktail in a Scarborough café, Brett asked Clare, "What did you make of our Dr Lipner, then?"

Clare put down her cold glass. "I never trust a man who doesn't take personal responsibility. Did you notice? He always used the royal 'we'. Hardly ever said 'I'."

"And?"

"It wouldn't occur to him that killing sea slugs might be wrong. A bad case of tunnel vision."

"He wouldn't have qualms about removing someone in the way of his skin cancer mission. Is that what you're saying?"

She nodded. "A real mean machine."

"What about you, Allen?" Brett enquired.

"I'll tell you one thing, man. His alibi's as leaky as

a snowball on Turtle Beach. Isabella McShine died at the weekend."

"Died? What from?"

Allen shrugged. "She was ninety-two. That's a good innings. But after Lipner's visit, she got sick. She complained of burning in her stomach, gut cramps and diarrhoea. Apparently, she was throwing up for a couple of days and having trouble breathing. A few convulsions and she was gone, according to her daughter. Pathology couldn't find anything. Just heart failure through natural causes. What do you expect at that age? No need for you guys to worry yourselves about it."

"Any checks for poisoning?"

"I'm not daft, you know," he replied scornfully. "I ordered every check. I got tests done here and in Trinidad. They didn't pick up any poison."

"Have you still got her body?" Brett asked. In Sheffield, the chief pathologist would never release a body until he had satisfied himself about the precise cause of death and decided whether a police investigation was warranted.

"There wasn't a reason to hold it back. It was handed over to the family. She was cremated and, I think, they scattered her ashes over the waterfalls in the rainforest."

Brett was still thinking about the old woman's strange symptoms. They puzzled and fascinated him. "Any punctures of the skin?" he enquired.

"Lots. This was a woman living in poverty in the

wilds of the rainforest. That makes you resourceful. She swore by folk medicine of all sorts. She injected herself with lots of potions from the forest. That's why she got to a ripe old age. Like a lot of folk up that end of the island, she didn't need a chemist shop."

"Mmm." Brett lapsed into silent thought.

In his car, Allen announced, "You got yourselves a real treat tomorrow. The Buccoo Reef trip with Fat Maurice. You're booked. I've taken care of it. Don't forget your hat and sun tan lotion, man," he said to Clare. "Remember, though, it's not all work. Enjoy. In fact," he said, twisting round in his seat and ceasing to pay any attention to his driving, "you can't not enjoy it." He laughed and turned back to the windscreen. "It's so good it'll make you forget the work. Just fill yourselves with the reef, Nylon Pool, then barbecue lunch, Creole style, on No Man's Land. I wish I was coming with you."

"Will you be on the case?" Brett asked.

Allen shrugged. "Doing this and that."

"This reef trip. When do we go and where from?"

"Pigeon Point. Just ask. Everyone knows where it is – or pick up a map from Janelle. You can go by car. A friend'll deliver a hired car tomorrow."

"Thanks," Brett said. "That'll help."

"Yeah, man. You can take yourselves off on a tour round the island as well. You stop at Jemma's Sea View Kitchen in Speyside for a West Indian lunch and sample her home-made lemonade. Heaven. Then check out the rainforest. It's a must. I've got a friend who'd be your guide. Very good. He used to be a botanist in the States but he dropped out of the rat race to work in paradise. That's a wise move."

"You've got friends who can fix anything," Clare observed.

"You didn't say the time for the reef trip," Brett reminded him.

"Ten at Pigeon Point but I wouldn't worry about it too much. I doubt if Fat Maurice'll be on time."

"Remember there's someone else we want to see," said Clare.

"Oh?" Allen pretended that he'd forgotten.

"Lee Teshier."

"Ah, yes. Lee," Allen replied. "Not today. He's out fishing. Tomorrow night at Crown Point Hotel, maybe. I'll let you know. But why do you want to bother him?"

Brett let Clare deal with Allen Rienzi. He was still musing on the convenient death of the person who could have incriminated Dr Lipner by denying his alibi. Or, of course, she could have cleared him by confirming his visit to her.

Clare was explaining, "Jason Lipner gets Teshier to do his controversial work on the reef – collecting sea slugs. He could have useful information. And perhaps Lee Teshier did even dirtier work for Xenox on the reef. He would've had his own reason to go along with the murder. Ellis had been intimidating him. He might want to remove the main objector to bio-prospecting because that would preserve his part-time income from gathering the sea slug harvest."

"But you forget, man. He wasn't around at the time. He was deep-sea fishing, miles away."

Clare nodded. "I know, but we like to look at every possibility – and check his alibi. There's Umilta McBurnie as well. We need to speak to her."

"First, you Brits take over our sea slugs, now you want to take over the investigation as well."

"Not take over," Clare insisted. "Just help."

"I'm more anxious than you to clear this case up. I've got a vested interest, man. This is my island. I don't want a killer roaming around. I want it solved. You probably think I'm doing it at a stroll but you're wrong. I just know how things get done round here. It takes time and patience to get the best information. I'm getting there – faster than any whiz kids."

To bring the friction to an end, Brett interrupted the exchange. "I assure you, Allen, we want it solved as well. Whether you crack it or us, it doesn't matter – as long as it gets done. Right now, though, I'd like to send an e-mail to my old tutor at Sheffield University, a Professor Derek Jacob. Any chance?"

"E-mail?" Allen queried with an absent expression.

"Yeah. It's like an electronic letter."

Allen guffawed. "Just checking if you think we're so simple in Tobago we haven't figured out computers yet." He laughed till tears came to his eyes.

Trying to extricate himself, Brett muttered, "I assumed computers aren't reliable in this humidity."

"Sure," Allen replied, wiping his eyes. "I'll take you to headquarters. You can do it from there. Then I'll run you back to the hotel."

When Brett and Clare went into their room, a harmless lizard that had been lounging in the shade scurried across the floor in a flash of green, under the patio door, out on to the balcony and seemed to dive suicidally off the edge. Really, it ran down the vertical wall with ease. On the left-hand wall of the balcony another lizard clung upside down, remaining absolutely still, playing dead. On the opposite wall, two multi-coloured monarch butterflies were displaying themselves. Down below, the red and green of the tennis court did not seem to have progressed much. The two young men were nowhere to be seen. Perhaps they were waiting for the evening when the temperature would drop to bearable.

Clare flopped on to the double bed. "Do you get the impression Allen's gone off to chase his own leads and leave us floundering in places he's already been?"

"We might as well enjoy it," Brett proclaimed. "How about a dip in the sea before dinner?"

Clare hesitated but then agreed. "I'll get changed and plaster myself in factor fifty-five."

They strolled down to the beach with just towels round their shoulders. Privately, they were both thinking the same thing. It was the anniversary of their partnership and they had never seen so much of each other. Living in the same room, working together… An outsider could easily take them for a couple. Even a married couple.

The water was almost a shock. In England, the chill of the sea was an unpleasant ordeal for the courageous or the foolhardy. Leisure was hard won. To enjoy it, fear of the cold and pollution had to be overcome first. In the Caribbean, the water was unexpectedly warm and relaxation easy. The hardest part was leaving the clear and welcoming water afterwards. Brett and Clare were both good swimmers. Brett was powerful but not so cultured. Clare was elegant and precise.

After a while of swimming alongside his partner, Brett stopped briefly to catch his breath. Ahead he saw something bobbing in the water. Clare was heading straight for it. He launched himself forward, grabbed her ankle and used his strength to pull her back. Spluttering and wiping the water from her face, she turned towards him and cried, "Hey!"

Brett pointed over her shoulder. The bright blue dome of a jellyfish wobbled on the waves. Underneath, long tangled tentacles dangled untidily. Buoyed by its gas-filled float, the creature moved at the whim of the wind and the tide.

Treading water, Clare turned back towards Brett and asked, "Is that what I think it is?"

"I'm no expert, but I think so. A Portuguese man o'war. The bits underneath would give you a nasty sting."

"Fatal, I heard."

"I think it's exaggerated," said Brett. "But it's not nice anyway."

"Let's turn back just in case," Clare suggested. Before breaking into a front crawl, she said, "You're not going to say this was put here like the spider – to put the frighteners on us?"

Brett laughed. "Not this time. You can't carry one of those around conveniently in a match box."

Clare put her hand on his shoulder briefly and said, "Anyway, thanks." Then she swam away.

Later, when the sun had lost some of its bite, they lay on their towels to dry off. Brett watched Clare wriggling her toes until her feet sank completely into the soft dry sand. There was no doubt about it. His partner was not just attractive. She had a bikini-friendly figure. Brett would not mind if holiday-makers mistook them for a couple.

That night they ate at the outdoor fish restaurant in Store Bay. Brett discovered a tangy vegetarian dish based on pineapple, mango and papaya while Clare talked endlessly about the sensational flavour of her grilled grouper in spicy sauce. At one point, all of the lights went out, leaving them in total darkness. The restaurant staff, experienced with power cuts, soon had three candles glowing on each table. Somehow, the meal tasted even better by candlelight. Across the road, some girls were playing loudly on the beach. Distant reggae music floated down the road. The sea lapped lazily on to the sand. The silhouetted heads of three swimmers broke the surface of the sea like huge jellyfish. Above, the stars stood out against a boundless black sky which was much more spectacular here than in Sheffield, where electric street lights obliterated the effect. The full moon's features were so clear it seemed to Brett and Clare that they could count the craters. It was easy to see why couples were so attracted to Tobago – or why Tobago made couples out of singles.

On Friday, Brett indulged himself at Buccoo Reef. He slipped on the rubber shoes and goggles, put the unfamiliar and unpleasant plastic mouthpiece of the snorkel into his mouth and lined up with the rest of the tourists to climb down the ladder from Fat Maurice's bright yellow boat. While Clare stayed in the shade onboard and sampled more of Maurice's supply of rum punch, Brett propelled himself towards the coral reef. He had come to see the fish that he had only ever seen before in aquariums.

Even among a bunch of noisy tourists, calling to each other to come and look at this or that, he experienced something of the wonder that had enchanted Ellis McBurnie. It was like swimming over an underwater maze. The flamboyant fish below him zigzagged expertly and effortlessly round the coral obstacles. Everywhere he looked there was something to astound. A pair of banded butterfly fish, a spotted red hind, spiky sea urchins, a shoal of grunts scavenging amongst a convoluted elkhorn coral. He decided simply to tread water and wait for the miracles to pass before him one by one rather than to try and follow a particular fish through the seascape. Besides, he couldn't keep up with their graceful twists and turns.

While he was stationary, ridiculously aggressive juvenile sergeant majors gathered round him. Striped black and yellow, they lined up and took it in turns to dart at his legs, trying to bite him with mouths so small that it was impossible. It was like a ludicrous attack by mice on an elephant. The coral teemed with spectral life. For every passing exotic fish that Brett could name, there were two that he did not recognize. He even thought that he spotted a *Dendronotus* nestling at the base of a pillar coral. The sea slug was a brown cancerous blob. The ugly duckling of the coral. Its unsightliness set it apart and somehow made it quaint, Brett thought. Among the ornamental, it was distinctive. And that made it pitiable and appealing at the same time. Brett wanted to support the underdog. He could have spent longer as a goggle-eyed spectator but Fat Maurice's whistle was a signal to return to the launch.

With the tourists congregated round the glass-bottomed section of the boat, watching the passing underwater world, Fat Maurice steered leisurely towards the Nylon Pool. For the benefit of the holiday-makers, Maurice's helper named the corals and vivid fish below the launch. His slightly slurred speech and large pupils suggested that he'd already sampled a lot of rum or that he'd taken something harder. But he was also well informed and witty. When he made exaggerated claims about the size and appetite of the local sharks, anyone who did not realize that he was joking would never go overboard again. Two French women kept on glancing at Brett – who had the best physique in the boat – and muttering quietly to each other. Clare noticed them and said to him, "I think you've got a couple of admirers."

"What a pity I've blown my chances," Brett quipped. "They'll think I'm with you."

Clare smiled. "That must be awful for you."

"Terrible." Then, suddenly serious, Brett said, "Actually no. Not at all." He took a sip of rum punch and looked vaguely abashed.

The salty blue water of the enclosed bay looked like a gently waving nylon sheet. That's why it was called the Nylon Pool. Its reputation for curing all manner of ailments had been nurtured by the tourist trade, not by the medical profession, but it was magnificent for relaxation. Treatment by unfettered floating. Clare soaked herself first in sun screen and then in the pool. On board, Fat Maurice turned his eyes frequently towards Clare as Brett spoke to him. "I guess Allen Rienzi told you why we're here when he booked us on this trip," Brett said quietly, out of range of the tourists.

"Yep," Maurice replied calmly. He didn't seem to regard Brett and the inquiry as a nuisance. He just didn't seem interested. He was distracted by his guests and the scenery.

Quizzing the reef guide, Brett found out that, despite his size, Maurice was an experienced swimmer and snorkeller but he did not dive. He slapped his folds of flesh and said, "I float too easy. Too much energy needed to get me underwater." He admitted that he had been at sea, near the reef, the previous Thursday afternoon but denied any involvement in his competitor's death.

Brett probed, "If the Government took away one Buccoo Reef licence, to stop that part of the reef getting spoiled, would it have been yours or Ellis McBurnie's, do you reckon?"

Fat Maurice rolled his head back and laughed loudly. "No doubt I'd have been OK." The tourist guide lived up to his name. He was enormous. Bigger than Big John Macfarlane. His bald head and chubby face rested on a swollen neck and from there his circumference increased till it stopped abruptly at the top of his thick legs. He was certainly not coy about his size. Quite the opposite. He used his larger-than-life figure and larger-than-life character to attract visitors to his trips. That was why he called his business unashamedly *Fat Maurice Tours*. That was why, when he stepped awkwardly into one of his vessels, he made sure that he had the maximum impact, rocking the boat alarmingly. He was an exhibitionist for the entertainment of the tourists.

"Why do you reckon the axe wouldn't have fallen on you?" Brett enquired.

"Because Ellis had another source of income: his university work. He was only a guide part-time, and a solo operator with only one boat. He did it for fun, not as a properly run business." Maurice talked as if he had nothing to hide. Or perhaps he thought that the investigation was trivial. "Me, I'm full-time, more experienced. Three boats I've got, and I employ helpers. The Government wouldn't have given the job to someone who just fitted it in round his other work, would they?" He stripped off the T-shirt that stretched over his mounds of fat.

Brett nodded. This jovial carefree man had a good point. "Do you know anything about medicine?"

Fat Maurice answered, "Enough to treat a fire coral or jellyfish sting. I got my training in first aid."

"Ever heard of thiopentone?"

Preoccupied with someone down in the water, Maurice grinned and stood up. Without even a glance at Brett, he said, "If it's a cocktail, I've never heard of it."

The interview had been brought to an end because he'd obviously decided to take a dip and no power on Earth could stop him. He had more important things to do than help a detective with an inquiry. He stood at the edge of the deck, his stomach hanging outrageously over his tiny swimming trunks. Instead of using the ladder like everyone else, he prepared to jump from the side of the launch. His colleague shouted, "Watch out below! Whale going overboard!" Maurice made no attempt to dive. He flopped to make as big a splash as possible. The boat lurched and Brett was saturated by the water displaced from the Nylon Pool by Fat Maurice's bulk.

Later, at No Man's Land, Fat Maurice waddled up the beach to some tables where his workers were grilling lunch under the palms that leaned over the sand. The aroma was exquisite and a portable CD player provided a fitting background of calypso.

Clare kicked off her shoes to feel the sand on the soles of her feet but immediately wished that she hadn't. The sand was on fire. It was too hot for barefoot walking. Donning her shoes again, she dived into the food and yet more rum punch.

Lounging under the coconut palms, Brett said, "You know, this laid-back approach to life could get infectious."

"You're beginning to sound like Allen," Clare observed. With her fingers she tucked into the barbecued kingfish and chicken in Creole sauce on an overloaded paper plate.

Along the stretch of sand, the CD player blasted dance music and Fat Maurice started a limbo dancing competition. He went first and, of course, failed to get under the bar at its first height. He made a great show of his clumsy attempt and absurd bungling. He looked more like a joker than a killer but how determined was he to prevent anything coming between him and his blissful lifestyle?

That night, over a meal at Crown Point Hotel, there was a surprise awaiting Brett and Clare. At first, they didn't take any notice of the steel band preparing to play by the pool. They talked about the case, Tobago, sun, spiders, sea slugs and skin cancer, past holidays: both disasters and delights. And they ate and drank.

When they looked at the group, issuing a few tentative notes to tune up, they were surprised to see Allen moonlighting – literally – in the steel band. "That explains it!" Brett exclaimed. "I bet it's not Allen the cop who's so well known and popular round the island. It's Allen the musician."

Next to Allen, the man who sold fruit outside the hotel every afternoon was fiddling with the microphone.

"Everyone round here's got two jobs," Brett murmured. "Fruit seller and singer, tour guide and marine biologist, police officer and musician."

Clare chipped in, "Musician and fisherman." She nudged Brett. "Recognize the chap on the left?"

Brett nodded. "You're right. Last seen next to a blue marlin in a photograph. We're seeing Lee Teshier in the flesh. Allen said we could catch him here."

Lee was testing the largest of the reclaimed oil drums, creating a deep resonant chime.

"No wonder Allen tried to put us off questioning him. He's a mate."

Fascinated, Brett and Clare watched the steel band. At the opening to each number they were ragged but, once they all started pulling in the same direction, their raucous rhythms were catchy and moving. After each heartfelt offering the reserved diners clapped politely when really the band deserved a spirited cheer. Brett and Clare did their best to raise the temperature by shouting approval. They'd finished their meal but sat and listened over a few more drinks. Clare threw back the alcohol, adding it to the free-flowing rum punch she'd consumed during the day.

At the half-time interval, Allen joined them for a cold drink.

"You didn't tell us you played in a steel band," Clare said to him.

"You didn't ask," he retorted. "Wednesday nights, we do Turtle Beach Hotel. Friday, Crown Point."

Brett complimented him. "It's good."

"At the height of the season," Allen told him, "we'll be at it most nights. During carnival, it's non-stop."

"Crooks on Tobago must feel like batsmen playing without fielders," Brett commented. "No one to catch them out."

"Not my problem, man. I take a holiday. Someone else takes care of the crime. Not that there's much. There's too much celebrating at carnival. Right now, it's quiet." Allen snorted disdainfully. "More reaction from the Americans."

"Quiet maybe," Brett responded, "but not crime-free."

Allen refused to be side-tracked. He dug a cassette from one of his pockets and slapped it on to their table. "We laid this tape down last week in the Tobago sound studio. Ten brand new tracks, every one a winner. You said we sounded good so you'll want it. To you, fifty TT dollars or nine US dollars. What do you say?"

Brett laughed and searched his pockets for a 50 TT dollar note.

Once Allen had taken the money, he remarked with a broad grin, "You should've haggled. I'd have come down to forty." He left them to prepare for the next set.

Two songs into the band's repertoire and Clare, decidedly drunk, stood up unsteadily. She said to Brett, "Come on. Dance time."

Brett surveyed the pool-side area. It wasn't really

built for dancing and no one else showed the slightest inclination. "Well…" he murmured doubtfully.

"Oh, loosen up." Clare held out her hand. "You might be clobbered by a mad axe-man tomorrow. Or a poisonous spider. So enjoy tonight – just in case."

Brett smiled and shook his head. "What the hell! We're on holiday. Sort of."

Almost immediately, the pulse of the calypso increased and the band played louder. There was added vitality and joy in the music. The musicians were thrilled that they had moved even the English, renowned for their reticence. Their eyes lit up and the rhythm pounded.

The owner of the hotel came out, watched the two revellers at the poolside and shrugged. He didn't have a licence for dancing but he wasn't going to stop them. With Allen Rienzi in the steel band, he'd be protected from prosecution.

Half of the diners watched the band. The other half watched Brett and Clare. The two detectives forgot about the audience, forgot their role as police officers on a murder case, forgot past casualties of their cases. They abandoned themselves to the swirling music and the heady tropical night.

Allen Rienzi urged on the band, improvising on a theme, and beamed at his English advisers. He had cracked them. He had made them succumb to Tobago's charm.

In her frenetic dance, Clare took a step too near to

the swimming pool. One moment Brett had a partner and the next he didn't. She hit the water, too intoxicated to make a refined entry. She splashed down like one of Fat Maurice's belly-flops. Luckily, she landed in the deep end of the pool and so she didn't crack her head on the bottom. She came up spluttering with laughter. After a hiccup in the beat, the steel band played on, realizing that she was unhurt and in good humour. Swimming to the side, Clare put up her hands. Brett bent down and pulled her out with ease even though, in sodden clothes, she was heavier than normal. Back on dry land, she fell into Brett's arms.

Brett held her for a moment and sighed with pleasure. Hearing the diners applauding their antics and beginning to feel his partner soaking him, he groaned theatrically.

Clare kissed him lightly, smiled and slurred, "Thanks." She was about to pull back from him but decided against. "You're right – we're on our hols." She hugged and kissed him again.

Then she carried on dancing as if her unscheduled dip had never happened.

At the end of the evening, when Allen came over to them, he said, "Moonlight and music bring out the angels – and the little devils – in us all. You two make a fine couple. I thought you were incapable of enjoying yourselves, thought you were addicted to work. But I underestimated you." He grinned at them and said, "It's a very romantic place, Tobago."

Their hotel was just along the road. A few minutes' walk. But it seemed to last a lot longer. They didn't hurry. They stopped by the wall and watched the sea and the outlines of diving pelicans. It was unspoilt and calm. Brett glanced sideways at Clare. He felt good to be beside her.

When they walked again, Brett stopped her stumbling and joining the frogs in the ditch by the edge of the road by guiding her with an arm round her shoulders. He didn't mind.

As soon as he opened the door to their room, Clare staggered in. For a moment, Brett lingered in the doorway, looking back into the night. The hotel grounds were quiet. Nothing moved. No one had followed them. Inside, while Clare sank directly on to one of the beds, Brett surveyed the room. Everything seemed to be exactly as they had left it. Even in a lazy tropical wonderland, murder made him wary.

It was Saturday morning. Brett went into Clare's room and asked, "Are you OK? Recovered?"

Still inert in bed, Clare merely groaned. But there was a trace of humour in her tone.

"Head feels like it's got a big brain coral inside?"

Clare turned on to her back cautiously, pulled down the sheet and moaned, "Worse." She exhaled and then exclaimed, "There's a man in my bedroom!"

Brett smiled. "Sorry. I was concerned. I had an

inkling you might need a bit of moral support this morning."

"Yeah. Good fun last night, though." A little embarrassed, she looked away from him for a moment and muttered, "Reckless." She sighed and added, "I think I used it to get something out of my system."

"Let's hope this morning your system doesn't let anything else out," he said. Really, Brett was joking to avoid talking about their flirting with each other. After all the months of regarding her solely as a team partner, he'd been shocked by the speed of the evening's developments. In the sober light of morning, he felt uncomfortable, wondering if Clare had already put it down to her emotional state or the alcohol. He'd lain awake trying to tell himself that was all it was. As police officers working together, that would be best. A hollow drunken encounter, easily forgotten. But, deep down, that wasn't what he wanted. He was joking because he didn't want to show he was scared that their sudden fling meant nothing. Sitting down on the other bed, he remarked, "It must have been a good night because, you know, we forgot we were supposed to be inter-viewing Lee Teshier."

"Ah," Clare murmured. "We ... er..."

"Got carried away. Forgot all about it." Brett hesitated and then said, "We relaxed and enjoyed a bit too much."

"That'll amuse Allen." Clare managed a fleeting

giggle and then, more earnest, began, "I … er… You and me, we…"

"Yes?"

"Are you sorry about … what happened?"

"Yeah," Brett replied with a sly grin. "Like I'm sorry when I miss a dentist's appointment."

Clare nodded knowingly and then ordered him out of her bedroom.

Before he put his shoes on, Brett checked them gingerly and carefully for eight-legged hideaways. This time there was nothing. In a way, he wished he'd found another sheltering spider. That would have meant it was a normal event on Tobago. If it wasn't, perhaps someone *had* arranged it. He kept his fears to himself.

The young men painting the tennis court had finished work for the week and, no doubt, would begin a frantic week's work again on Monday. At breakfast, a waiter brought Brett and Clare a note from Allen. It read, *Nothing doing till Monday morning. Take tour of island.* They laughed. While Brett delved enthusiastically into the cocktail of fruits, Clare sipped a black coffee delicately.

Up above the banana plantation, the rainforest was bursting with life. Enormous bamboos, land crabs, snakes, trees, termites, frogs, wild parrots and innumerable birds heard but not seen because of the thick foliage overhead. Below, leaf-cutting ants followed a trail across a muddy path, like well behaved nursery school children going into a classroom in a line. The ants staggered under the weight of their loads. They carried fragments of leaves far bigger than themselves as if they had grown large green fins. Rain hit the canopy above Brett and Clare and provided a permanent drizzle beneath. "Refreshing," Clare said, celebrating the cool wet atmosphere in the fertile forest. "Good cure for a hangover."

"Wonderful," Brett agreed. Then he confessed, "I had a quick look in the phone book at the hotel. While you were in the shower, I called round the hotels. I know where Jason Lipner's staying. And I called the police. They gave me directions to the place where Isabella McShine's daughter lives. Both are on our route today. I checked on the map while you were driving. When we leave here we could…"

"Take the opportunity to ask a few more questions, I know. But tell me, Brett," she asked, "would you have *chosen* to come to a place like this for a holiday?"

Brett nodded. "It's fantastic."

"And with me?" Still feeling fragile and yet elated by the rainforest, Clare halted and looked at her partner.

"No competition when the alternative's Big John Macfarlane," he teased. Then he took her hand and said, "No, I can't think of anyone better to share it with. And I'm glad you haven't forgotten last night. Glad it wasn't just the booze." He hesitated, looking down at the hand in his, before adding, "It wasn't just the effect of … the last case and Liz, was it?"

"Liz was very complimentary about you, you know," Clare remarked in a tone that suggested she was revealing forbidden secrets. "A girl could do a lot worse, she said." She squeezed his hand.

"Very complimentary," Brett muttered. Running his free hand through his hair, he was surprised how wet it became. "When we get back out into the sun, we'll steam," he said.

"No hurry," Clare replied. "You know how much I appreciate hills, shade and rain. Reminds me of Sheffield."

Brett pointed at a branch where a long snake was basking in the mist. "Never seen that sort of thing in Sheffield." He rested his hand on her shoulder and asked, "Homesick?"

Clare laughed. "Only for the weather."

Mrs McShine's unmarried daughter was virtually destitute. Evelyn McShine shared a shack at the perimeter of the rainforest in Speyside with her house-bound brother. The place had the sweet scent of a mixture of herbs. The roof was made of huge dried leaves from banana trees. It was a pity that Evelyn's mother had not lived long enough to sell her folk cure to Xenox. The family could have used a donation from a rich pharmaceutical company.

Evelyn McShine was very distrustful towards the white police officers but responded better to Clare than to Brett so Clare took the lead. "You could really help us with an inquiry, Evelyn. You see, there's a chemist who Allen Rienzi thinks might have killed a local man. This chap from Xenox says he came to see your mother. Did she have a visitor just before she became ill?"

Evelyn shrugged.

"Did she say anything about someone calling?"

"A white man from England?" Evelyn mumbled.

"Yes. That's why we're looking into it. He's a British national."

"He killed one of us?"

Patiently, Clare replied, "He might have killed someone on Tobago, yes."

Evelyn let out a long weary breath. "Things don't change."

"Pardon?"

Evelyn shook her head. "By the time I got to Mam, she was beyond saying anything much. She was delirious." While she spoke, she avoided looking at the English detectives.

"Delirious?" Clare prompted, hoping to hear more now that Evelyn was answering questions.

"Mam treated herself with … something from the forest. Something to make her feel better, to take the pain away. She was out of it."

Clare enquired, "Did she say anything at all?"

"She only said about being sick. Stomach, burning throat, bad breathing. I think something in her callaloo upset her."

"Callaloo?"

Evelyn sighed at the newcomers' ignorance. "It's a

type of soup. She made herself one most afternoons. Okra and dasheen leaves – like spinach – boiled with chicken bones for flavour. Now and then, she'd add a flower to make her hot. More often, a different flower to make her cool."

Sometimes, Brett was thinking, it's difficult to tell the difference between food and therapy. Surprising Clare, he followed up with an unusual question. "Did your mother ever use castor bean seeds in any of her concoctions?"

Shocked, Evelyn wagged her finger at him. "Bad. Very bad. The seeds are poisonous. Mam wouldn't have them in the house."

"Interesting," Brett murmured. Breathing in the almost intoxicating smell and wondering if it came from a herb that Evelyn used to ease her brother's condition, Brett said, "I guess your mother passed her … art on to you?"

Her eyes narrowed with suspicion and she answered his question in a begrudging voice. "I'm not as skilled as she was but she told me some of her remedies."

"Has anyone from Xenox visited *you*, asking about them?"

"Me?"

"Yes. A white man." Brett assumed that, if Dr Lipner was really keen on learning the old wife's tale, it wouldn't be beyond his wit to seek out surviving relatives in case they had the same knowledge.

"No one's been to see me – apart from police,"

Evelyn replied impatiently. "And you."

There were a number of possible explanations for Jason Lipner's absence. Maybe he had been with Isabella McShine on the afternoon of the murder, just as he'd claimed, because he wanted her medicinal secrets but, after she died, he did not think to pursue her daughter instead. Or maybe he thought that a second attempt so soon after Isabella's demise would be indecent haste. It was even possible that Isabella *had* told him everything he wanted to know, even though he would not admit that she had. But there was another possibility. Perhaps Jason wasn't interested in her potion at all. Perhaps he had invented a fictional trip to Isabella McShine and instead killed Ellis McBurnie. Afterwards, he'd arranged her illness and death so that she could not disprove his alibi. If so, Isabella McShine could not have known that she had been poisoned because if she had she would have struggled through her pain to tell her daughter.

On the other side of the island, Brett and Clare visited the rambling and luxurious complex of Mount Irvine Bay Hotel, built on an old sugar plantation. It was one of the most expensive places to stay on Tobago and had its own golf course. That was where they found Dr Jason Lipner. On the thirteenth green. Brett strode towards the pharmaceutical chemist and said, "I can see you're busy so I've only got one more question. What type of frog was Mrs McShine using in her wound treatment?"

Jason squinted at Brett and frowned. "Is this some sort of test?"

Brett did not need to be elusive. He was blunt. "Of course."

"Well, I hate to disappoint you, Inspector Lawless, but we don't know. I assure you I'm not lying. I *was* with Isabella McShine but she wouldn't reveal her sources, as journalists say. My guess is that, if I'd had the chance to go back to her with a bigger offer, she'd have been more ... co-operative. I didn't get that chance." He paused to watch someone tee off on the fourteenth.

"There's still no proof you had that Thursday afternoon chat with her."

"There should be," Jason replied. "I left her my business card. Note that it's not exactly the normal behaviour of some crook up to no good."

"True," Brett agreed. "But this isn't normal. If you went to her place later than you claim, you could have left the card then. It doesn't prove a thing."

As Brett walked away with Clare, he said, "I wonder what search powers Allen's got. I'd really like to turn the Xenox lab upside down – to see if they keep a supply of thiopentone or anything that would kill Mrs McShine without leaving a trace."

On Tobago, Sunday mornings were very quiet. Everything shut down while the population migrated to the island's churches. The place seemed deserted. The locals began to emerge again in the afternoon. That was when Wilton Cipriani found Clare lying in the shade of a thatched umbrella on Store Bay beach. He knelt beside her and prompted, "Bracelet?" Then he reminded her, "On Wednesday you said, 'Some other time.' It'd make you even more beautiful. Your man would like." He glanced at Brett lazing on the sand.

Brett smiled at his description but he chose not to comment on it. Instead he said, "I wouldn't dare interfere but she looks good in anything."

"Very tactful," Clare said with a grin. Turning to Wilton, she said, "Oh, why not?" She chose a bracelet with the colours of the sun, grass and blood.

"The yellow sun feeds the green grass," Wilton explained in his strange drawl. "Grass feeds the animals. Animals feed us. They give us red meat and red blood." Without giving Clare a choice, he began to fasten the bracelet round her wrist himself. Then he looked directly into her eyes and said, "There. The colours of life." Mysteriously he added, "It'll bring life, lady."

When Brett volunteered to pay the beach trader's exorbitant price, Wilton held out a handful of CDs and tapes and said, "The best American music, going very cheap. You want?"

Brett shook his head. "Just the bracelet, thanks."

Clare held up her arm and said to Brett, "Well, what do you think?"

"Cute," he replied. "Suits you."

Then, for twenty minutes, it rained. Huge drops of warm rain. The·thatched cover provided shade from the sun but it was too small and low to shelter the tall detectives from the downpour. Brett and Clare could have run for better cover and cowered for the duration of the deluge but there wasn't much point. It wasn't unpleasant like dull cold British rain. It was welcome relief from the heat. Instead, they opted for bravado. They did not even attempt to keep dry. Rather, they decided to get so wet that rainfall made no difference. They plunged into the sea. The grass beside the beach, feeling the impacts on its open leaves, curled up and played dead while secretly guzzling the life-giving liquid. At once, the sand turned a darker shade of orange and the surface of the sea became mottled with countless expanding rings. When the deluge suddenly stopped, the immediate sunshine dried the puddles of water in half an hour. Soon after Brett and Clare emerged from the sea, the warmth also dried them.

On Monday morning, Allen was still thinking about his English colleagues' antics on Friday night. "You didn't see the *No Dancing* sign, then?"

Brett answered, "No."

At the same time Clare admitted, "Yes, but I didn't take it too seriously."

Warming to his visitors at last, Allen said to Clare, "I like your attitude, man. If you weren't such an awful colour I might make you into a local yet."

Allen had called them into police headquarters because Brett's e-mail from Professor Derek Jacob at the University of Sheffield had arrived. Allen handed over a hardcopy of the message and said, "It's about a Bulgarian writer." He allowed Brett and Clare time to read it without interruption.

Brett. In your e-mail, you were right about Georgi Markov. He was a dissident Bulgarian writer assassinated in London in 1978. It is a fascinating case. He became ill after being jabbed with a poisoned umbrella while waiting at a bus stop. The poison was never found but a small metal pellet had been injected into his leg.

The pellet had a hole for the poison to leak out. Analysis of tissue samples and the pellet cavity did not reveal anything. One of the very few poisons that are lethal at levels that cannot be detected is ricin. So it was assumed to be ricin. It comes from the seeds of the castor bean (grown commonly in tropical climates).

Markov's symptoms: burning sensation in the mouth, throat and stomach; sickness; diarrhoea; abdominal cramps; convulsions; breathing difficulty; death.

You also wanted examples of marine bio-prospecting for cancer drugs. I found three. To get 1mg of an anticancer drug, one group harvested 450kg of the acorn worm. I also have a reference to 2400kg of a sponge having been removed from its natural habitat to isolate 1mg of another anticancer drug. Similarly, 1600kg of a sea hare has yielded 10mg of dolastatin which shows some promise for treating skin cancer. That's a lot of marine life sacrificed for new drugs. On average, the extraction efficiency is about 0.0000001% by my calculations. It's rough being a biologically active organism.

PS. You owe me a holiday in the Caribbean but I will settle for a postcard and a pint. Minimum.

"I read the list of symptoms," Allen admitted. "They're remarkably familiar. You reckon Isabella McShine was poisoned with ricin from seeds grown in the West Indies."

"The e-mail doesn't prove it but, yes, it's a real possibility," Brett responded. "I thought her symptoms rang a bell. Thought it might be the famous poisoned umbrella case in London. Real James Bond stuff. It stuck in my mind."

Allen said, "You're pretty good at this game."

"You're just saying that because you like the way we danced to your music."

Allen laughed. "Yeah. Fancy footwork there as well. And I'm saying it even though you came here to help me solve a murder and all you've done is give me another one."

"I should've warned you about Brett," Clare said. "With him, things usually get pretty complicated before they're sorted out. Remembering your school science lessons helps. But bear with him and he gets there in the end."

Brett mentioned their visit to Isabella's daughter and ended by saying, "She was a bit wary of us, actually."

"Only wary? Not hostile?" Allen exclaimed. "I'm not surprised. Without me there, you're lucky she talked to you at all."

"Why?"

Allen sat down with a thud. "We're strong Christians here, we believe in forgiveness. But we can't forget our history, either. Ever since you sent us Christopher Columbus, whites have fought over the island and taken us for slaves." He hesitated and then declared, "That's bio-prospecting as well, you know. Our ancestors were treated no better than sea slugs, kept in captivity to help white-skinned people. Whole tribes were wiped out – with less thought and reason than for the harvesting of *Dendronotus*. Some people find it hard to forgive that sort of cruelty."

Clare was nodding sadly. "It's amazing that so many people here are so friendly to us. So willing to share the place with outsiders."

"History lesson done," Allen said. "We live in the present, not the past. We've got nothing against modern tourists – not unless they bring crime."

"Have you got anything else on Lipner?" asked Brett, thinking that Allen was dropping a hint.

"Nope. But there's something I ought to mention about Umilta McBurnie," he said. "I think I know who she was with on Thursday afternoon. She wouldn't say but word on the island is that a certain politician might be getting himself into hot water by dating a married woman. It doesn't go well with the voters if a politician's having an affair with a man's wife at the very time he's murdered."

"Haseley Abidh?"

"Uh-huh. The one and only. A journalist friend of mine got a long-range fuzzy picture of a woman on his yacht a few days before the killing. It could've been Mrs McBurnie. No problem."

"We're still waiting for that interview with Umilta McBurnie," Clare reminded him.

"I know," Allen replied. "I'll sort it out when I can, man. This afternoon or tomorrow. We'll see how it goes."

Brett decided to make the most of Allen's talkative mood. "You said Abidh wasn't at work last Thursday afternoon. Where was his yacht?"

"All I know is it wasn't moored in the harbour."

"So he might have been out on the high seas when Ellis died," Brett concluded. He thought for a moment and then asked, "Did you find Jason Lipner's business card at Isabella McShine's place? He claims he left one."

"Uh-huh. But it doesn't prove a thing, man."

Brett smiled at the repetition of his own words.

Clare joined in, saying, "Allen, on Friday night we were going to talk to Lee Teshier but ... we didn't get round to it. I know he's your mate but he's got to be on the hit list. He's got plenty of motive for wanting to see the back of Ellis McBurnie. What do you think?"

"Yeah, he's got a bagful of motive," Allen replied, "but, nope, he's in the clear. I know where he caught his blue marlin. He couldn't have got back to the reef by mid-afternoon. Besides, I know Lee. No way. Music and murder don't mix, man."

Surprising both Clare and Allen, Brett enquired, "Can we trace the owner of a yacht called *Katarina*?"

Allen looked puzzled. "*Katarina*. For sure. I'll put one of my people on to it. Why?"

Evasively, Brett answered, "I saw it near Xenox. Just wondered who it belongs to." Really, he'd seen the name in the newspaper article that Clare had spotted. It was written on the yacht behind the record blue marlin. In truth, Brett was testing Teshier's alibi but, because Lee was Allen's friend,

Brett felt that a lie was justified. If anyone was on the yacht at the time when the photograph was taken, they would be able to confirm Lee Teshier's triumphant return with the titanic fish. "And talking of Xenox," Brett added, "wouldn't you just love to get in there and take a look around? See if they've got any thiopentone or ricin. Or anything else that would kill Mrs McShine at very low levels."

"Relax," Allen said, smirking and spreading his arms wide. "You two aren't the only ones round here with brains. I've already applied for the warrant." Suddenly, be added, "Hey, I bet you guys have never ridden a police launch. Want to come?"

"Where? What for?"

"Buccoo. Because it's a nice day."

"It's always a nice day here," Clare replied. "Is this your way of inviting us to see where McBurnie died?"

"You catch on quick, man," Allen said on his way to the door. "And you never know who you might bump into at Buccoo marine park."

The boat hummed with power but Allen did not open up the throttle. He was content to cruise lazily. Gently buffeted by the slight swell, the waves hardly rising up the hull of the craft, they coasted towards the coral reef. In the shade of the bridge, Clare shook her head, let the wind ruffle her hair and then replaced her hat. "This is the life," she said. "Better than crawling round Sheffield ring road, choking on the exhaust fumes."

Nearing Buccoo Reef, Brett and Clare looked back

at the mainland, two miles behind them. "Long way to swim," Brett murmured.

Clare agreed. "But," she replied quietly, "I could do it, so I bet quite a few islanders could."

A small fishing boat was anchored at the edge of the reserve. Steering towards it, Allen remarked, "Lee's here. You can make up for missing him on Friday night. No problem."

Brett nodded knowingly. He did not doubt for a moment that Allen had wangled this meeting and that he would have primed his friend for the questioning. Brett expected only well rehearsed answers from Lee. Nothing useful.

Swimming to the police launch and hauling himself up the ladder, Lee pulled off his snorkel and greeted Allen as if their encounter had not been stage-managed. Then he turned to the South Yorkshire detectives and said with a smile, "The British dancing team. Excellent!"

Brett took off his shades, congratulated Lee on his part in the bewitching music and then nodded towards the reef. "Getting sea slugs for Xenox?"

"Dr Lipner called this morning. He pays me peanuts but it all helps." While Lee talked, water ran down his muscular and glistening body.

"Not waiting for the permit, then?" It was almost an accusation.

"You're off target. Xenox needs a few more slugs, that's all, see. We're still waiting for the verdict on mass harvesting. I won't jump no gun."

Brett asked about Lee's activities last Thursday and the massive blue marlin.

"I wasn't nowhere near here, if that's what's on your mind," Lee answered. "I set off early morning for the deep fishing waters west of Grenada, a hundred and fifty miles away, see. I didn't get myself back till early evening – only just in time to catch enough light for the photo that went into the paper," he added proudly.

Allen snatched up a pair of binoculars and gazed out to sea, while Brett continued with his questioning. "Do you know a woman called Isabella—?"

But, with more gusto than he had ever shown before, Allen interrupted, "Time to break this party up, Lee." He jerked his thumb to the north and muttered, "Police business."

Unquestioningly and without complaint, Lee made for the ladder and scrambled down it. He seemed relieved. As soon as he'd cleared the boat, Allen set off at an electrifying pace. The prow lifted over the waves as the launch accelerated to top speed. Brett grabbed the rail and Clare grabbed Brett to stop themselves staggering back. Above the noise of the motor at full revs, Brett cried, "What's up?"

"Unless I'm seeing things," Allen shouted, "we've got another floater."

"Another what?"

"Not so much bitten the dust as tasted the saltwater. Another body."

10

Allen cut the engine and Clare removed her sunglasses and hat. Together with Allen, she jumped overboard and manhandled the inert body to the steps at the side of the craft. Above them, Brett took hold of the victim's limp arms and yanked him out on to the deck. Kneeling beside the white man, Brett's fingers searched for a pulse in his wrists and neck. Then he bent down and put an ear to the man's chest. "Still warm but ... nothing detectable."

Allen brushed Brett aside, saying, "Dare say I've seen more drownings than you." Immediately he tilted the drowned man's head back, checked his mouth for obstructions and then breathed directly into him four times in quick succession. After that, he began regular deep breaths every few seconds. He looked up at Brett and Clare and said, "Anyone confident to give heart massage?"

Clare volunteered. "I'll do it."

"Try not to break his ribs, man," Allen said with a wry smile.

Clare knelt at the man's side and placed the heel of her left hand on his chest and her right hand on top of that. She pushed downwards firmly using the weight of her shoulders. In rhythm with Allen's attempted resuscitation, she tried to coerce the man's heart into beating. One chest compression every second.

The launch drifted while Brett watched the attempts to revive the man they'd hauled out of the ocean like a big diseased fish. Brett examined his unresponsive fingers and said, "Not very wrinkly. Hasn't been in the water for long." Aged about fifty, with close-cropped hair, he was clothed in T-shirt and shorts. His face and legs bore several nasty bruises like the flesh of a battered apple. Brett suspected that he had been severely beaten up before being dumped overboard. Using Allen's binoculars, Brett scanned the ocean for other vessels. The large ferry from Trinidad was sailing past Sandy Point on its way to Scarborough. There were a couple of motorized yachts in the distance. Neither was close enough to identify. A small yellow launch was in view, pottering about near the tourist part of the coral reef. The police vessel might be the fastest craft in view but they could not use it to chase the other boats. With the rescued man still flat out, they could speed only to the hospital.

"Let me take over," Brett suggested to Allen. "I can't drive this thing. You can. I'll keep him going and you get us back to dry land."

"OK," Allen agreed.

As they swapped positions, Brett enquired, "Do you know him?"

"No." Allen started the motor and steered a direct course back to Scarborough.

Clare whispered to her partner, "Second body to turn up in a place Lee goes to a lot."

"Firm alibi for the first," Brett remarked briefly between exhalations.

Clare kept her voice down so that Allen would not be able to hear above the noise of the lurching boat. "*If* he's telling the truth. If someone else didn't do the marlin catching for him." Plainly she had not been convinced by the fisherman's tale. "I'd like to hear what people near the fish saw. Like Lee driving up to the quayside to take the credit for the catch."

"I'm working on that," Brett admitted. He filled the man's lungs again with his own breath and explained quickly and quietly, "The *Katarina*'s the yacht that was moored behind the blue marlin."

"Ah, good." Clare rested for a few seconds from the relentless pounding of the limp stranger's breast-bone and then applied her weight to him again. The bracelet on her left wrist dangled on to his chest. She looked at Brett and said, "Let's hope Wilton was right. Let's hope this bracelet *does* bring life."

As the shuddering police launch surged past the

ferry, Allen turned towards his British colleagues and shouted, "Anything?"

Both of them shook their heads.

"Keep going," Allen urged them. "You don't give up on drownings till a doctor pronounces them dead. The body can shut down for half an hour, just keeping a trickle of blood and oxygen to the heart and brain. You never know. You're all that stands between him and a premature place in heaven." He radioed ahead for a trauma team and an ambulance to meet him at the harbour side.

Neither Brett nor Clare were optimistic but stubbornly they continued their joyless and exhausting task of supporting a brittle life – if there was any life at all.

The sea breeze and sun had dried Allen, Clare and the unconscious man by the time the boat approached the quayside at reckless speed. Allen spun the wheel expertly and used reverse thrust to bring the launch to an abrupt stop perfectly alongside the wall. Immediately, three paramedics jumped down into the boat and took over from the amateur first-aiders. In a well practised drill, they yanked up the man's shirt and attached electrodes to his chest. After a few seconds of watching a monitor, one of the emergency team shouted, "We may have a life here. But he's dead if we don't bring him back now. Stand clear!"

Brett and Clare climbed up from the launch and out of the way as a paramedic passed an electric shock through the victim's chest like a crazed Frankenstein triggering life in his dormant creature with bolts of lightning. Nothing. "Again," someone shouted. The machine delivered a punch that could jump-start a truck. But would it jump-start a human life? The man's body jolted cruelly as if he'd been shot. But the effect was the opposite of a bullet. A technician cried, "That's it. We've got a pulse!"

The trauma team didn't let up. Talking to each other continuously, they busied themselves with small vials, syringes and injections into their passive patient. It looked like chaos but the medics were following a rehearsed routine. As soon as they had stabilized the man's heart rhythm with drugs, they lifted him on to a stretcher. While two of the paramedics manoeuvred him towards the ambulance, the other said to the police officers, "Good work. You kept him in the land of the living."

"But will he be OK?" asked Brett.

The medic shrugged. "Depends if his brain got starved of oxygen. He could recover completely, or he may never even be able to say thank you." Then he whisked the casualty away in the ambulance.

Allen, Brett and Clare followed in a separate car. At the hospital, Allen took a phone call. Afterwards, in the waiting room outside the intensive care unit, he said to Brett, "That yacht – the *Katarina* – belongs to one Dominic Harper, an American businessman originally. He's in the filthy rich league. His Florida recording business rakes it in. He bought himself Tobago citizenship, though. He built the island's recording studio – the one that my band uses. The deal was, Harper lets local bands use his facilities for next to nothing and he attracts the big American stars here to record their albums in peace and quiet. In return he got a Tobago passport. A bit of back-scratching and international co-operation. On top of that he married a local girl. Name of ... Abidh. Yes," Allen stressed, "he's Haseley's brother-in-law."

"Very interesting," said Brett.

With a grin, Clare asked, "Is everyone on the whole island related to each other?"

"Just about," Allen answered. "It's a small community."

"Anyway," Brett said, "I think we'd better go and have a word with Dominic Harper." He stood to one side as a porter came past with a patient on a trolley. "Look, I don't like fibbing to you – or anyone else. What we're doing is checking Lee Teshier's alibi," he confessed to Allen. "This *Katarina* was berthed next to Lee's boat when he was photographed with the blue marlin."

Allen's expression turned into an uneasy frown. He opened his mouth to reply and then changed his mind. Instead, he said, "Well, at least you're honest. I ought to... No. You go and see what you can find out." He reeled off Harper's address and then said, "I'll work on our friend's identity." He inclined his head towards the closed door to the emergency room. "And I'll get someone back out on the waves to check up boats in the area."

"For one thing, the big Trinidad ferry was out there," Brett said. "Any chance of a list of passengers?"

"You've got to be joking, man! It's run like a bus."

"Pity."

"If nothing's happening here at the hospital," Allen continued, "I'll set up a team to search Xenox."

Back in their hired car, Clare said to Brett, "At least Allen's letting us help now. He's pulling with us rather than against."

"Yeah," Brett replied. "And we know why. Because you let your hair down. Metaphorically speaking." He glanced at his partner and said with a grin, "It was a good ploy."

"You know it wasn't just a ploy."

He put down the map of Tobago. "Yes, I do know."

Dragging Brett back to the investigation, Clare reminded him, "Allen's got a journalist friend who snaps pictures. The one who photographed a woman on Abidh's yacht. Maybe this photographer does other work for Allen and his friend, Lee Teshier. Like photographing big fish. If we don't get anything out of Dominic Harper, the photographer could be a good source of information. We could trace him – or her – through the newspaper offices."

Brett nodded. "Good idea. We'll check out Harper first and then see if we need more."

Dominic Harper's property was an old rambling colonial house of whitewashed wood surrounded by lush grounds. The gardens contained a swimming pool, a tennis court and a huge number of different species of palms. A hammock was suspended between two of the trees. Once, the maids, butler, housekeeper and cook would have been called slaves but Mr Harper treated his domestic staff well. Even so, in a poor country, he could bind them to him with the meagre salary that had replaced the manacles of the past.

In the spacious reception room, surrounded by the carvings and relics of African slaves, Brett did not even finish the introductions before Harper interrupted, bellowing, "Hey, you're English! English police working on Tobago. That's real quaint. What you doing here?" He was a stout man, considerably shorter than both Brett and Clare. He was about forty, with an extravagant American accent, dressed in outsize shorts and a casual but classy shirt.

"We're looking into a serious crime. With the full authority of the Tobago Police Force."

"And if I choose not to answer your questions?"

Brett shrugged. "You might as well. If you don't, I guess the locals will come out and ask you themselves. You're not under investigation yourself..."

"I should think not, boy!"

Brett continued, "But we believe you might be able to assist us."

"How's that?"

Clare chipped in, "Cast your mind back to the week before last. Thursday. Your yacht, *Katarina*, was moored in Scarborough. Were you on board in the late afternoon?"

While she spoke, Dominic looked her up and down as if he were examining and assessing a sculpture. "Very nice," he murmured to himself. Then, answering her question, he said, "You got your facts all wrong, my dear."

"Detective Sergeant Tilley," Clare informed him forcefully.

Dominic switched his gaze to Brett and smiled at him as if another man should understand and automatically take his side. For a moment, Brett thought that the objectionable American was going to remark, "She's a wilful little thing, isn't she?" His expression certainly said it. Brett scowled at him and kept quiet to allow Clare to carve him up if she felt like it.

Clare decided not to antagonize him until she got the answers that she wanted. As politely as possible, she enquired, "In what way are our facts wrong?"

"I was sailing with my wife, north end of the island, all day Thursday. So, whoever told you I was moored in Scarborough is up to no good. It's a matter of mischief or appalling memory, I'd say. So, I can't help you, I'm afraid."

"When *was* your yacht moored in the harbour that week?" asked Clare.

"Only Wednesday, August six. I arrived in the

afternoon, loaded up with … supplies, moored over-night and set sail next morning. That's your lot."

Clare glanced at Brett and then said, "Did you see anything out of the ordinary in the harbour on Wednesday?"

"Now you got to help me out here, my dear. Like what?"

"Like the press arriving for the landing of a fish."

"Oh, that," he replied. "Yes, one of my staff suggested I take a look. Someone was showing off a real bitch of a sailfish – or was it a blue marlin? – I always have trouble telling the difference."

"And you're sure it was the Wednesday?"

"Certain. You don't get on in business without knowing what day it is." He burst into disproportionate laughter.

Clare responded, "I still need to confirm it. Who was this member of staff? He or she would be able to put our minds at rest about the day. It's very important."

"Aw, you don't need to do that. You got my word for it."

"You don't get on in police business without checking your facts," Clare stated.

Dominic paused, uncertain about how to react to her barbed comment, and then decided to grin. But it wasn't whole-hearted. He didn't like Clare's cheek. Even so, he relented. "I hire a local guy – name of Wilton Cipriani – to load the boat. He's the one who called me on deck to check out the fish."

"Wilton," Clare repeated. "We know him. Tall. Beach trader."

"That's the fellah," Dominic said.

To Brett, Clare muttered, "Another one with two jobs."

Brett nodded and then turned to Harper. "Do you know where he is now?"

"No idea, boy," the American replied. "Selling things to tourists on one of the beaches?" He nodded his head in the direction of Wilton's bracelet on Clare's left wrist.

"OK," Brett said. "Thanks for your time."

"That's it?" Dominic queried. "What's going down? Just what are you investigating?"

Clare looked him up and down and barked, "You don't get on in any business by giving away trade secrets."

As they walked to the door Brett tried unsuccessfully to suppress a triumphant smirk.

In the car, they both sighed. They needed to confirm Harper's memory of the day of the colossal catch. "We need to find Wilton. A tour of every beach?" Clare joked.

"Has its attractions," Brett replied. "But…"

"The newspaper office? Bound to be in Scarborough. Chase the photographer," Clare suggested.

"I guess so," he agreed. "And it'll take us back towards Allen and Xenox."

But when they found the newspaper's

headquarters, no one could help. The press had bought the blue marlin story and photograph from a freelance reporter called Kiera Jeffers. And no, no one knew where she was right now. Pursuing some human interest story, no doubt.

Brett and Clare headed for the hospital and, on the way, agreed that they wouldn't confront Allen with the evidence against his friend, Lee Teshier. Not until they had confirmed that Lee's alibi of the blue marlin was in fact nothing but a red herring. In the event, they did not have to evade Allen Rienzi's questions. He had left the hospital because the news on the rescued man was bleak. He was still in intensive care. The doctor had also spotted a head wound that would have concussed the patient. He would not be in a fit state to talk for at least twenty-four hours. A message from Allen told Brett and Clare that he'd gone to organize the search of Xenox. He would meet them there at four o'clock. At the end of the note, Allen had scribbled, *No ID in our wet friend's pockets but clothes are American. I've got people working on his ID, checking with hotels, etc.*

"Right," Brett said. "We've got three hours. Time for that tour of the beaches. How about starting with lunch at Store Bay? The tourist guide in the hotel says Miss Esme's cooks the best food in the area, including vegetarian."

"Now you sound even more like Allen," Clare replied. "He'd be proud of you."

They were lucky. They found Wilton at the third attempt. He was showing his wares to German tourists near Pigeon Point. When he noticed the detectives, he exclaimed, "Ah! Allen's British friends. Good to see you again, even if you are cops. Have you changed your mind about the CDs?"

Both Brett and Clare would have shown more interest in the compact discs if they had been local calypso music. It seemed to them a waste to come all the way to Tobago and take away American pop and rock CDs that were available in any airport or record shop back home. "No," Clare replied. Using the unhurried approach like a native, she said, "Just here for a chat and to buy a drink." She surveyed the beach for a shack.

"There's no need to buy a drink if you don't want

to," Wilton told her. "Nature provides." Mysteriously, he walked away, disappearing into the private estate behind the beach where long curved palms grew. The scene adorned a thousand holiday brochures and postcards. After a few seconds he returned with a green coconut. "Here, this is more a drink than a fruit." He drew a knife from its holder at the back of his trousers and sliced off the top of the coconut with ruthless efficiency. He held it out to Clare as if he were offering a can of Coke. "Fresh milk. Drink. It's good. Very refreshing."

While Clare tipped up the shell and drank, Brett commented, "Nature doesn't provide everything round here. Who provides the CDs? They haven't fallen off the back of Dominic Harper's yacht by any chance, have they?"

Wilton looked hurt. "What does that mean?" But almost certainly he knew.

"Harper trades in music recordings. You sometimes work for Dominic Harper, we hear, and you sell cheap CDs on the beaches. Are they stolen?"

"No way!" Wilton drawled. "I sell them for him. Most go to the US but Mr Harper keeps a few for sale here. He gets his cut and there's a percentage left over for me."

With a smile, Brett quipped, "All above-board, then. Good." Out of curiosity, he asked, "But why are they so much cheaper than normal?"

Wilton shrugged. "That's Mr Harper's price. You'll have to ask him."

"Never mind," Brett replied. "We wanted to ask you about something else." He took the coconut offered by Clare so that he could share its milk.

While her partner drank the cool drink, she said to Wilton, "I want you to think back to the week before last. Thursday. Did you load up the *Katarina* with supplies and see a giant blue marlin?"

Wilton was surprised by her interest. Hesitant, he answered, "Er ... yes. Yes, I did. But I think you'll find that was the Wednesday."

"Can you be sure?" Brett asked eagerly.

"Yeah. Because it was Lee Teshier. As soon as he flashed his teeth next to the fish he dashed off to Turtle Beach Hotel. You see, he plays—"

Brett interrupted. "In Allen Rienzi's steel band. Every Wednesday and Friday."

"You got it," Wilton said. Then he was distracted. Hungrily, his eyes followed a large group of English tourists as they strolled towards the picturesque jetty.

"It's all right, Wilton," Clare said to him. "You've helped us. A lot. Thanks. You can go and get yourself some more customers." Before he trudged out of earshot, Clare called, "And thanks for the coconut."

Wilton looked over his shoulder and shouted, "You're welcome, lady."

There were several cars and a van outside the Xenox building by the time that Brett and Clare arrived. The search had already begun. Compared with any search conducted by the police in England, it was a curiously lax affair. Pairs of gloves were the only protective clothing on show. No one had taken a video recording of the premises before the examination. There was only a photographer waiting to take stills of any significant finds. As far as Brett could tell, no one was taking a register of everyone involved in the search.

The Xenox staff had been bundled from the premises but Jason Lipner had been kept back, out of the way in his office. Allen was standing in the middle of the activity like a lazy lord, surveying the search but doing nothing himself. Brett asked, "Anything interesting yet?"

Allen shook his head. "There's stacks of chemicals and bits of marine life," he said, "but nothing eye-catching."

Brett went to take a look. The forensic team had lined up all of the chemical containers on the benches and shelves. Brett walked along the rows as if he were inspecting troops. Most of the very large bottles contained solvents. Perfectly innocent for a chemistry laboratory. The lesser bottles made from dark glass were used to store more specialized substances: starting materials and reagents. The smallest containers were sample tubes containing home-made chemicals. They had been labelled correctly according to safe laboratory practice. No sign of barbiturates or ricin. Brett looked at Allen and shook his head.

Brett noticed two wretched specimens at the end of the bench. Out of water, lying on a cold laboratory slab, *Dendronotus* looked even more pitiable. These two smelly lifeless lumps had obviously failed another attempt to get them to live in captivity. Now, they were waiting to be dried, powdered and processed for their precious poison. The sea slugs had been snatched from their idyllic habitat and dumped into a drab tank that could not sustain them. They were victims of humanity's hunt for health. All of a sudden, Brett felt despondent.

Ten minutes later a gloved forensic scientist held up a small vial from the back of one of the cupboards and called for Allen. "What is it?" Allen queried.

The technician pointed at the label on the bottle and said, "Thiopentone. And it's been used."

"Get it dusted for prints," Allen ordered straightaway. Then he strode directly into Lipner's room. "You told us you didn't keep this thiopentone stuff," he said.

"We don't," the chemist insisted.

"So why have we just found some in your laboratory? That's pretty damning, man."

Dr Lipner's mouth opened, closed and then opened again. "Well, I assure you it's not mine. And I don't see why any of my staff would…"

Allen laughed. "At this point, you're supposed to claim, 'It's a plant!' That's what everyone else does."

"I don't know about that but it's got nothing to do with me, Officer Rienzi," Jason stated. Thinking quickly, he said defiantly, "Has it got my fingerprints on it? Because if it hasn't you can't prove it's got anything to do with me."

After a few minutes, Allen had the answer to Dr Lipner's question. The fingerprint specialist reported that the bottle of thiopentone did not have any dabs on it. Not even a partial. Allen sighed. Without prints, he did not have an unarguable connection between Lipner and the murder weapon.

The search continued but nothing else of significance surfaced. Allen did not have a firm basis for arresting Jason Lipner, even though a strong case against him was beginning to form.

Allen spread out the menu in front of his colleagues and tapped the extensive section on fish. "Flying-fish burger. That's what you want, Clare. An imaginative combination of West Indian and American culture. Swilled down with a Carib, it's beautiful – and cheap."

Over the meal, they discussed the case. Interrupted only by the usual succession of people greeting Allen like an old friend, they talked about each suspect in turn. The most obvious was Jason Lipner. "He's certainly got a motive," Clare remarked between mouthfuls. "Removal of a protester who threatened his livelihood."

"A man who wouldn't let the drug trade benefit while marine ecology suffers," Brett added.

"And Lipner's alibi went under along with Isabella McShine," Allen added. "He may well have been the last person to see her alive." He bit into his burger like a hungry shark with flashing white teeth.

"There's something else, Allen," Brett put in. "He called Lee Teshier this morning, to get him to collect a few more specimens. But what else might he have organized with Lee? Teshier may be your mate, but he was close to our drowning victim. Through Lee, that gives Jason Lipner a connection to all three casualties. Our only suspect with such good connections."

Allen objected, "But the floater might have nothing to do with the McBurnie case, man."

"Granted," Brett replied. "But there's another problem with Teshier."

"Oh?"

Getting directly to the uncomfortable truth, Brett said, "He caught his blue marlin on the Wednesday, not the Thursday like the newspaper reported."

Clare added, "We agree Lee's got an alibi but it's for Wednesday the sixth. Someone – probably Lee himself with the co-operation of the reporter – tinkered with the date in an attempt to provide an alibi for Thursday the seventh."

"That must mean he's got a good reason for wanting an alibi," Brett concluded. "Otherwise he wouldn't have risked it. He's in deep, Allen."

"Are you sure about this?" Allen asked.

They both nodded. "Certain."

Allen Rienzi looked first at Clare and then at Brett. He exhaled deeply and then said, "Who did you speak to after seeing Dominic Harper? Wilton Cipriani, Kiera Jeffers?"

"You knew about it!" Brett cried.

"Some days, you want to throw in the towel and become a full-time musician instead." Allen shook his head. "Sorry. I nearly said something before you went to Harper's place but … I thought you might not find out because he'd be hazy about dates. And I knew you wouldn't take just one man's word for it anyway. That's why I know you've spoken to someone else to be so sure."

"But what's going on, Allen? In England, it'd be called perverting the course of justice. Serious stuff."

"Yeah. I knew Lee manufactured his alibi with Kiera's help. Let's face it, it's not the coolest deception you'll ever come across. A bit of digging around and I was bound to see through it. But I didn't blow his story open – I looked the other way – because he's not our man. Believe me, I know Lee. And Lee knew he'd get away with it. He knew I'd bowl underarm. Why waste my time asking too many questions when he's clean?"

Cutting in, Brett asked, "Well, what *was* he doing on that Thursday afternoon? Why did he need to hatch this plan to get himself an alibi?"

"He was out fishing locally," Allen said. "On his own and not a huge distance from the reef. That's why he got scared when I told him McBurnie had been killed. If he'd told the truth it'd look suspicious. So, he was making it easy for me, doing me a favour."

"Doing *you* a favour? What do you mean?"

"He knows I have to write reports and stuff. I'd have to put him down as a suspect because he'd clashed with McBurnie. He'd got a motive and opportunity. So, he gave me a little something for the report. He decided to buy a little insurance by switching the date of his marlin catch. Nice and neat and easy. If he was nowhere near Buccoo, he was in the clear. No problem." Allen leaned towards his colleagues and said, "Don't get me wrong. I'm not covering up for him. I'd book him if I thought ... But Lee wouldn't do anything like murder. No way."

Brett replied, "Maybe he wouldn't – normally. But, from what you just said, he was near Ellis McBurnie when he was poisoned and we know he was near our mystery floater. He was collecting sea slugs under Lipner's orders. What else was he doing under Lipner's orders? Perhaps the Xenox man's got some sort of hold over him. I don't know. Blackmailing him to do his dirty work. To me, it looks grim for Lee Teshier."

"A Lipner and Teshier double act," Allen muttered. "We heard from your English boss you were the imaginative sort: the one who comes up with exotic theories. Relax. As I said, we don't even know if the floater's got anything to do with it. But I'll tell you one thing. Lee hasn't got a connection with Isabella McShine."

Brett retorted, "We don't know if *she's* got anything to do with it, either. She was an old lady.

Maybe confused. She was into herbal remedies and the like. Maybe she confused one seed with another. Maybe her death was nothing more than an accident. Self-poisoning."

"No chance, man. If she was prone to accidents, she wouldn't get to ninety-two. The only obvious link is to Jason Lipner, not Lee."

"Agreed. But it's not a simple link. It could work in Lipner's favour or against him. Maybe he invented the afternoon talk with Isabella but killed her later so his alibi can never be disproved. Or maybe it was real and someone else got rid of Isabella so Lipner's alibi can never be *proved*."

Allen ventured, "He's still the one with access to chemicals and the knowledge to use them. And he's still the one with the most to gain from McBurnie's death."

"Mmm." Brett pondered on it and then replied, "Maybe. But we don't know enough about some others yet."

"Others?"

It was Clare who answered. "Haseley Abidh. We need to look into him – pronto. And Umilta McBurnie. She could stand to gain quite a lot. Like a new life with someone else. That's powerful motivation. I'm still keen to speak to her."

"And I don't want to forget Fat Maurice," Brett put in. "After speaking to him, I'm not convinced he's got an obvious motive but he *was* out on the sea when Ellis was killed. I might have spotted one of his boats at the reef today as well. And I don't think he's as dumb and easygoing as he likes to act."

Allen said, "I've already done Fat Maurice and Mrs McBurnie – straight after her husband turned up dead. I know you want to try your luck as well but I'll take a back seat."

"Why do you say that?" asked Clare.

"Come on. If Umilta McBurnie and Abidh have got a thing going, I'm leaving well alone. Abidh's the sort of man who can get me the sack." Looking at Brett, Allen said, "Would you investigate your own boss and his girlfriend?"

Brett did not answer. His mind went back to his first case when, against Big John's orders, he did investigate his own Detective Chief Superintendent and his wife – and, yes, it did get him into trouble.

"I'll tell you what we need most," Allen continued.

"What's that?" Brett prompted, taking a gulp of cold beer.

"We need our floater to come round and tell us who he is, what happened and who did it. We can't do much without his ID."

"Well," Clare said, "that's in the lap of the gods – and the doctors. We can't do anything for him so I suggest we get going." Supporting her partner, she stressed, "Umilta McBurnie and Haseley Abidh in particular."

Allen smiled. "No rush, man. It'll be dark soon. Tomorrow's another day."

12

Once some noisy Italians at the bar had retired for the night, the poolside area at Tropikist became tranquil. There was a hush that Sheffield could not match, even in the middle of the night. Side by side, Brett and Clare swam leisurely up and down the pool, relishing the emptiness. Taking a break, Brett floated on the water and surveyed the sky that was bloated with stars. He felt as if he were drifting in some spacecraft with the humdrum affairs on Earth a hundred light-years away. "Sheer luxury," he muttered to himself. Then, treading water, he said to his partner, "An evening off. Not bad, eh?"

Clare smiled. "You wouldn't want it like this all the time. Not if it was your case. You'd run around like mad, day and night, if you were in charge. So engrossed in the chase, you'd forget time. You're an answer junkie. Can't rest till you get one."

"And you'd do it with me," Brett replied, swimming to the shallow end where they could stand. "But, remember what John said. We're on holiday as well. In one of the most romantic places on the planet." He held out his right hand and remarked, "All sorts of things can happen on holiday that'd never normally happen back home."

She took his hand and gazed at it for a moment. "Why *does* skin go wrinkly in water, Brett?"

Brett laughed and clasped her other hand. He said, "You're putting off the inevitable. Why? Because of your career. You're worried because the powers-that-be frown on partners who become something more."

"I *was*, yes," she admitted. "But maybe Liz taught me something – we're here today and tomorrow we might not be. Anyway," she whispered, "it's not just me holding back. Not just career or what's right and wrong for us. I might as well say it. You still blame yourself for the death of a witness, a woman you – how shall I put it? – got to know." Clare hesitated to let Brett reply but he said nothing. There was just a hint of a nod. "It was a year ago, Brett. Time to let go, to forget." Forming a doleful smile, she declared, "Let's face it, as a team we're pretty good but, as a couple, we're riddled with hang-ups."

Brett sighed and looked down at her hands in his. He paused before saying, "It's got something to do with having layers of skin. The outer ones absorb more water and expand more. The extra area's taken up by crinkling. Something like that anyway."

With an ironic grin, Clare shook her head. "There goes the inevitable."

On Tuesday morning, they interviewed Umilta McBurnie in the house that she had shared with her husband. The property had nothing in common with hovels like the McShines' and none of the grotesque opulence of Dominic Harper's mansion. It was a comfortable, neat one-storey home, furnished with quality goods. The paintings on the wall were not to Clare's taste but they were originals and the work of local artists. They depicted in rugged realism the beaches, streets, villages and shanties of Tobago. At opposite ends of the lounge there were outsize loud-speakers. The stack of hi-fi equipment was lavish and, next to it, there was a huge collection of CDs. Along the opposite wall, shelves held innumerable novels, biographies, books on art, biology texts and a large framed photograph of Umilta and Ellis.

Mrs McBurnie herself was as attractive as Allen had claimed. She was a short woman in her thirties but looked much younger. Asian in origin, she had wide brown eyes and shiny black hair that reached down to the small of her back. She wore a long loose dress of red silk. She moved serenely, as if gliding, and sat down. She waved her hands towards more chairs as an invitation to the detectives.

After Allen had explained why the British officers

had been invited to Tobago, Clare said, "Mrs McBurnie, I'm sorry we're having to bother you at a difficult time but there are a few questions... Did you support your husband's campaign to keep Xenox off the coral reef?"

Unperturbed, Umilta answered, "I believe the reef is not a candy store for humans to pick and choose from. It has to be protected, yes, but Ellis did exaggerate the threat sometimes." She paused and then added, "In my view."

Clare was surprised by the woman's composure and the cultured precision of her language. Nothing like the informal style of most of the other people she'd met on Tobago. "Did he suspect that Xenox might try to get rid of him?"

"Certainly he did. And it seems that is exactly what has happened."

"Do you have a definite reason for saying that or is it just a feeling?"

Umilta replied, "As I told Mr Rienzi, it's what I believe to be true."

"It must be strange, here on your own," Clare observed. "How long were you married?"

"Seven years."

"Will you be moving?" Clare had the vague impression that the small house did not suit Umilta. She had the air of a caged princess. She might well have designs on a more up-market home. Perhaps she believed that she deserved something like Dominic Harper's palace.

"I do not have a crystal ball, Sergeant Tilley."

"Were you with your husband when he died?" Clare enquired. "Or in the boat."

"No," Umilta responded briefly.

"You were doing … what?"

So far, Mrs McBurnie had maintained a warm, untroubled smile and her eyes shone. Now, though, her expression changed. She declared, "I did not kill my husband." She made the pronouncement so forcefully that it was very difficult to doubt her.

"I was looking for a witness," Clare claimed, "not a culprit. But I'd still like to hear where you were on the afternoon of Thursday the seventh."

Umilta glanced at Allen as if expecting some protection but it did not come. "I believed I had an understanding with Officer Rienzi on this uncomfortable question. I was with someone else: a man whom I would not care to name because it would cause him embarrassment."

"We have to know who he was," Clare persisted.

"I have no wish to hinder your investigation but I cannot understand why this is important to you. It has been hard enough for me to admit that I was seeing another man. I give you my word that is where I was – to my shame." Umilta shifted in her seat and turned her imploring eyes on Brett.

Resisting Umilta's unspoken appeal, Brett explained, "We need to know not because we want to embarrass him but because he had something to gain from your husband's death. You."

"If you're implying that he killed Ellis, your logic is faulty. He was with me that day."

Shrewdly, Brett did not argue the point. "Yes, that's true," he replied. "Do you love him?"

With her head held high she stated, "Yes."

"Then as far as we know you might be protecting him from an accusation of murder, not just embarrassment. Unless you name him so we can check him out, you could be telling us you were with him solely to give him an alibi."

"I am still reluctant..."

"Right now," Clare put in, "neither of you has a proven alibi. Let us talk to him and it's likely you'll both have one. Simple."

Umilta shook her head.

Deciding that he would have to play rough to get a name from her, Brett said, "We'd be much more discreet if we didn't have to ask around for a man who might have been seen with you that day."

Umilta stared at the carpet for a while and then looked up. "Now you are not leaving me much choice."

The three police officers looked at her in silence.

Again, Umilta flashed a look at Allen. Seeing no hope of a reprieve, she said, "I take you at your word. I expect you to be discreet. I was seeing Haseley Abidh."

"OK. And *where* did you see him that day?" asked Clare.

"On his boat. And before you ask, we were

nowhere near Buccoo Reef. We were off the north end of the island, away from prying eyes."

"Will you continue to see him?" Clare enquired.

A trace of disdain came to Umilta's dazzling face. "I will think about that only after a decent period of mourning."

Clare nodded. "Of course."

Excusing himself, Brett asked if he could use the bathroom. Once Umilta had directed him towards the right room, Clare said, "When you were sailing up north with Mr Abidh, did you see anyone else? Like his sister and Dominic Harper on their yacht?"

"I believe I saw the *Katarina* once – in the distance."

"What time would that be?"

"I'm not sure. Mid-afternoon. Possibly about three o'clock."

Clare changed the direction of the interview. "Do you have a career, Mrs McBurnie?"

"I own two shops selling West Indian art, mainly to tourists."

Clare glanced at the walls. "Hence the paintings."

"Indeed."

"Do you know Isabella McShine?" Clare queried.

"I know of her. I'm told she died soon after my husband. I sympathize with her family."

"Do you know anything about her?"

Umilta shook her head. "Nothing."

Clare could believe it. At the opposite ends of sophistication, the two women were not in the same league. They hardly seemed to belong to the same country. They were worlds apart. "Have you ever come across castor bean seeds?"

Umilta frowned. "No. Why? Does this have anything to do with my husband?"

"Only indirectly." Clare did not want to explain so she plunged into the next question. "Do you know anything about barbiturates?"

"Very little. They're sleeping pills, are they not?"

"That sort of thing." Suddenly guessing why her partner had gone to the bathroom, Clare continued, "Do you – or did your husband – keep any here?"

Brett came back into the lounge just in time to hear Mrs McBurnie deny it. She said, "We are – were – very fit and healthy. We have no use for medicines – of any sort."

Brett remained on his feet. "Well, thanks for persevering with us. You've been very helpful. I don't think we need to worry you any more for now."

Outside the house Clare nudged Brett and, with a grin, murmured, "Dodgy bladder, is it? Or a swift rummage in her medicine cabinet?"

"She was telling the truth. Nothing more serious in there than paracetamol."

"Well," Clare remarked, "I bet she's got the phone in her hand already. A minute more and Abidh will know everything about this little interview."

Both Brett and Allen nodded in agreement. "We're not going to get an independent story from him. I'm sure, by the time we get to him, his version will be beautifully in tune with hers."

"Hang on, you two," Allen said. "Fair play. Their stories'll match if they're simply telling the truth. It doesn't have to mean they're telling the same lie to cover up a murder."

"Truth or contrived lie? Innocent or guilty? Two opposite theories. Either way, we get the same neat story." Brett smiled. "No one said this was an easy job. I'll tell you something else. There's a third possibility. They might be perfectly innocent of murder and still have a good reason for lying. Abidh's got his reputation to think of. So, even if we did catch them telling fibs, they might be lying just to stop a scandal cutting short his career."

"You won't like this, Brett, because it's just a feeling," Clare interjected, "but I believed Umilta when she said she didn't kill Ellis. And it seems she was yachting miles away at the time."

"I'm tempted to say the same," Brett responded.

"She was just as convincing when she said she'd had nothing to do with Mrs McShine – though you were bursting to get to the loo at the time."

Brett chuckled. "What do *you* think, Allen?"

With a big grin, the enchanted police officer said, "Don't ask me, man. Umilta McBurnie could persuade me I'm an Eskimo."

Shortly after, when Allen received a telephone call to say that Mr Abidh had managed to find a slot for the detectives that very afternoon, none of them suspected coincidence.

The politician from the Trade Department held out his hand towards Brett but almost immediately withdrew it so that he could cover his mouth as he let out an explosive sneeze. He did not repeat the offer of a handshake and he did not allow the police officers to take the lead. Articulate and intelligent, he took charge of the conversation straightaway. "Now, I understand you've interviewed Mrs McBurnie this morning. And you applied considerable pressure to her at a time when it strikes me she should be allowed to grieve for her loss. Anyway, what's done can't be undone. She was coerced into telling you that she and I share some private time together. I trust that you'll be tactful with this information."

Before Allen could reassure the man who could

make or break careers in the Tobago police force, Brett jumped in. After all, an English policeman could not be touched by a West Indian politician. "We're as tactful as possible, given that we're pursuing a murder case. And we can be *very* tactful if people are helpful and honest with us."

In the corner of the office, Allen cringed.

Haseley Abidh's desk was awash with papers, folders, fax messages, a laptop computer, two telephones, a beautiful glass paperweight in the shape of a dolphin. It was the dominion of a busy man. He was approaching forty years of age, Clare judged, and he was certainly more handsome than Ellis McBurnie. Clare believed that she sensed a playboy behind his air of stern authority. She could easily imagine him throwing off the formality of his office, his suit and tie, and enjoying himself with an attractive woman.

To take the wind out of Brett's sail, the politician declared, "Despite the ... unpleasantness of the McBurnie case, I hope you're enjoying our island."

"Very much," Brett replied politely.

"Good. We wouldn't want your stay to be brought to a premature end." Before Brett could respond to the threat, Haseley said, "Now, what did you want to ask me?"

"I'm sure you realize that the death of Ellis McBurnie might be linked to Xenox's intended harvest of sea slugs from Buccoo Reef Marine Park. Is the government going to allow it?"

"The decision will emerge quite soon." Haseley had the practised vagueness of a politician.

"Which way will it go?" asked Brett tenaciously.

Haseley laughed. "I can't discuss that before announcing it to my colleagues!"

Brett repeated himself. "I did say we're discreet if people are open and honest. After all, we *are* dealing with an extremely serious crime that your Government wants to clear up before it affects the tourist trade."

Abidh sighed and then made up his mind. "We're very keen to bring Xenox business to Tobago for the benefit of the island economy."

Allowing himself a little outrage on behalf of the sea slug, Brett said, "So that means you're putting economy before ecology?"

Surprised by the implied criticism, Abidh argued, "I'm walking a fine line between the two. We're not a rich country – you'll have noticed – so we encourage investment wherever we can. But we also have to protect our natural resources because that's what brings in the tourists and tourists are our bread and butter. Here, we were influenced by the fact that the commodity is a sea slug. Tourists don't flock to Tobago specifically to see *Dendronotus*."

Getting the interview back on track, Clare asked, "Is the decision to allow the sea slug harvest known outside this building?"

"No. And I expect it to stay that way until I make the official announcement." He flashed a glance at

Allen Rienzi as if he was making the local detective responsible for keeping the secret.

"News hadn't been leaked – not even to Umilta McBurnie?" Clare checked.

"No. I keep my role as a public servant and my private life apart."

Brett realized that his partner was pursuing a crucial point. If Xenox knew that the permit was about to be granted, Jason Lipner and his workers would not have had a motive for removing their chief opponent. To be sure, Brett enquired, "At the time of Ellis McBurnie's death, twelve days ago, did anyone know the decision?"

"Not even me," Haseley answered. "The matter was only resolved on Friday and the formal processes haven't been concluded yet. When Dr McBurnie died, there was still everything to play for. We were still listening to the arguments for and against."

"OK." Brett was satisfied that Lipner still had a motive. "Now, talking of the time of death," Brett said, "I've got to ask you where you were on the afternoon of Thursday the seventh."

Abidh leaned forward on his crowded desk. "You know where I was," he growled.

"Let me put it another way," Brett said. "For Mrs McBurnie's sake, can you confirm that you were with her?"

"Even though I find your question distasteful and tactless, I can. We were sailing north – away from Buccoo."

"And would anyone have seen you?"

"We tend to steer away from the crowds – for obvious reasons," Haseley responded, looking at his watch.

"Did you see the *Katarina* or speak to your sister?" Clare enquired. "She was in the same area on Thursday."

"It's a big ocean, Sergeant Tilley. We saw a few craft in the distance. One might well have been the *Katarina*."

The ocean might be a big place, Clare was thinking, but she was not totally convinced by Haseley's hostile reply. If Abidh and his sister and brother-in-law had been out on the waves at the same time, it seemed likely to Clare that they would have made radio contact at least, unless Haseley was keeping his entanglement with Umilta a secret even from the Harpers. Clare tried a different line of inquiry. "I suppose, like everyone else round here, you're a good swimmer and diver?"

Allen winced. At least Abidh was not in a position to fire *her* for impertinence.

"Of course," the politician responded. "And since everyone else *is* the same, there's no adverse implication."

Brett asked, "What, if anything, did you do before you were a politician?"

"I worked in business. That's why I now find myself in Trade." He turned his head away from his visitors and sneezed again.

Clare smiled and said, "You're pretty unlucky to go down with a cold in a place like Tobago."

Haseley did not see the humour in his affliction. "It's not a cold. I have a few allergies, I'm afraid."

Brett was wondering if the politician had gained any medical or pharmaceutical insight from his past. "What sort of business did you work in?"

"I owned a hotel and a health club. Before that, a long time ago, I trained at the University of West Indies, taking a course in business studies."

It seemed unlikely that this background would give him the working knowledge of medicine and biochemistry that the killer obviously possessed. Brett asked, "Did you know Isabella McShine?"

"Only by reputation," Haseley answered. "I understand from Dr Lipner that Xenox was showing an interest in her medications. It's a pity they didn't cotton on to her skills long ago, when she still had a few years left in her. She could have done well out of it if Xenox had found some interesting substances in her concoctions."

"All right, Mr Abidh," Brett said. "Thanks for your time."

"I take it that Mrs McBurnie and I will be left in peace now?"

Brett stood up. "Certainly. As much as the investigation allows anyway."

Haseley stared at Allen and commented, "I'm sure you'll do all you can not to involve us again."

Outside the House of Assembly in the lively

Scarborough street, Allen said, "I suggest you get in your car and follow me."

"Why?"

"Because there's someone I think we want to speak to. A friend of mine."

Brett nodded. He was pleased that Allen was now including them in his plans.

They drove in convoy to the north–eastern district of the capital and pulled up outside a brick-built house. Getting out of his dented car and leaving the door wide open, Allen strolled up to his friend's home. Brett and Clare joined him there but no one answered his big fist on the front door. "He's not in," Allen said. He turned round and waved towards the edge of the road. "If he was around, his jeep'd be parked here."

"Who is he?"

"Sonny Bourne. I'm not sure if Sonny's a child-hood nickname that stuck or his real name. It doesn't matter. He's Sonny to everyone."

"And why did you want to talk to him?"

"Just a minute," Allen said when he caught sight of a neighbour. He walked over to speak to her. When he returned, he looked puzzled and concerned.

"What is it, Allen?" Clare asked.

"He hasn't been seen for a day or two. That's not right for Sonny. I'm putting out a call for him. I'll get a light aircraft up to look for his jeep."

"You've got a helicopter?"

Allen laughed. "This isn't some rich British police

force. I've got a friend who owes me a favour and who's got a small plane. No problem."

"Is there anything you can't do with the help of one of your friends?" Clare said.

"What are friends for?"

Brett asked again, "Why did you want to see Sonny Bourne?"

"He's the rainforest guide and botanist I told you about," Allen replied. "Maybe I'm wrong but I reckon, years ago, he told me he collected natural foods and folk medicine for a health club. It could have been any of the clubs, though."

Brett nodded. "But you're wondering if it was for Abidh's and, through Sonny, Haseley Abidh found out about castor bean seeds and ricin. A botanist would know all about them."

"Sonny was friendly with Isabella McShine as well, so Abidh might have known about her by more than just reputation. That's what I'm thinking."

Suddenly, Brett uttered a quiet curse at his own shortcomings. "I'll tell you what. You search for Sonny while we go and ask Jason Lipner a vital question I should've asked him ages ago." Brett shook his head. "The holiday mood must be getting to me."

"Whatever you say, man. You speak to Lipner. I'm going to take a look round the house." He nodded towards Sonny's front door. "And then I'll get airborne."

They found Dr Lipner back at his hotel. He had

finished a round of golf and was sipping a lurid cocktail by the open-air bar. Joining him, Brett remarked, "Not at work, then?"

Jason sighed. "If only. This whole damn business is so disruptive. Right now, Rienzi's people are grilling my colleagues. We can't get any work done under such circumstances."

"You can practise your swing, though."

Bad-tempered, Lipner said, "What do you want, Inspector Lawless?"

"You can tell me how you knew about Isabella McShine and her frogs."

"I told you. Word just gets around that an old woman is renowned for ... you know ... providing certain substances for every occasion." Jason hesitated and then recited, "*And in her needy shop a tortoise hung, an alligator stuffed, and other skins of ill-shaped fishes.*"

Recognizing the quotation straight away, Clare replied, "The chemist's shop in *Romeo and Juliet*. Almost."

Trying to keep to the point, Brett said, "You make her sound like a witch. Or drug dealer."

Jason grimaced. "That's putting it a bit strong. She used nature. That's all."

Clare chipped in with her own bit of Shakespeare. "*Eye of newt, and toe of frog, wool of bat, and tongue of dog, adder's fork, and blind-worm's sting, lizard's leg, and owlet's wing, for a charm of powerful trouble, like a hell-broth boil and bubble.*"

Smiling, Jason said, "Now that *is* over the top. Mostly, she cured various ailments."

"But who told you where she lived?" Brett enquired. "Who fixed up your meeting with her?"

"Why?"

"Because whoever it was might be able to back up your alibi."

"If you don't accept my word, yes, I suppose he could. Well, it was a mutual acquaintance – a botanist called Sonny Bourne."

"Ah." Brett looked for a moment at Clare. "He's a rainforest specialist. I'm told he collects folk medicine, like Isabella. Did you use him at all?"

"Use him?"

"Just like Lee Teshier gets your marine samples, does Sonny Bourne get rainforest specimens for you? Or, like Ellis McBurnie, does he object?"

"We didn't use him a lot…"

"Didn't?"

Jason corrected himself. "All right. We *don't* use him a lot. I said *didn't* because he got us samples in the past, not recently."

"He didn't object to plundering natural sources, then?"

"Sonny's got a practical, sensible attitude about using what the environment provides *and* conserving it. He strikes a sensible balance."

Brett said, "It's a pity, then, that a man who could clear you has disappeared off the face of the island. That means both people who could confirm your version of events, Sonny Bourne and Isabella McShine, are out of commission. A convenient coincidence."

"Not convenient for me!" Jason cried. "It'd only be convenient if I was lying but I'm not. I'm telling you the truth. Anyway, what do you mean, he's disappeared?"

Brett shrugged. "Exactly that. Have you got any idea where he is? If you *are* telling the truth, it'd help your cause to find him."

Jason shook his head. "I don't know anything about it. I don't know why these people are falling like flies. I can only imagine it *is* coincidence – or someone's got something against me, trying to discredit me."

"Who'd do that?"

"No idea." He paused before adding, "A friend of Ellis McBurnie perhaps, or whoever it was who killed him."

"Where were you yesterday morning?"

Dr Lipner stared at Brett in horror. "Not another ... incident?"

Brett had no intention of telling him about the man who had nearly drowned. He simply repeated the question. "Where were you?"

"Any of my team'll tell you. I was at work."

"In the lab? Not at the reef?"

Jason smiled. "On dry land – where I prefer to be. Surprising as it may seem to you, I don't like going out on boats. I prefer solid ground beneath my feet."

"Spoken like a true son of Sheffield. I can tell you're not native to Tobago. Do you swim or dive, then?"

"Both. It's the motion of boats I can't stand."

"Well, you can't come to Tobago and not go snorkelling or diving," Brett said. "It's compulsory."

"Mmm." Jason refused to be drawn into a dangerous conversation about swimming at Buccoo.

"You called Lee Teshier, though."

Lipner looked up and squinted at the sun over Brett's shoulder. "I didn't know that was a crime."

"You got him to go to the reef reserve."

"For a dozen *Dendronotus*," Jason said. "Nothing more."

Brett took a deep breath of clean Caribbean air, looked at the deep blue sea and then glanced down at the chemist again. "It's nice here. Anyway, thanks. That's the lot for now."

As they walked away, Clare giggled. "You know, for a second there, I thought you were going to do an Allen. 'It's nice here. Relax. Enjoy. Time we were taking it easy as well.'"

Brett put his hand on her shoulder. "I told you. His laid-back approach to life is catching."

Opening the door of the car, Clare said, "Before you grind to a complete halt, let's slip back to the hospital. Pay a visit to our resurrected victim."

Brett nodded. "Good idea."

14

"What's your verdict on the man who heads our hit list?" Brett enquired.

Clare pondered on it for a moment as she negotiated the worst pot-holes in the road. "Lipner's shifty. Could be telling the truth. Could be fibbing brilliantly."

"Yeah. No question about the motive, opportunity and ability to poison McBurnie and Isabella McShine."

"Plenty of questions about his alibis."

Brett looked skywards at a small plane flying towards the north. "I wonder if that's Allen."

Clare nodded. "I bet it's nice up there." The car bumped over a raised drain and Clare said, "Car springs don't last long here, do they?"

They met some resistance at the hospital. The

consultant in charge of the recuperating patient told them, "He's a very lucky man. He's going to be all right. And, yes, he's conscious now, but Officer Rienzi left very precise instructions. *He* would be the first to speak to the patient. No one else."

Brett smiled. "I think he was referring to members of the public, casual visitors. He didn't mean us." To remind the doctor that they were police officers working with Allen, Brett showed his British warrant card.

The consultant shrugged. "Means nothing to me. As far as I'm concerned, you *are* members of the public."

"OK," Clare said. "If we can't speak to him, do you have any information about him? Like his name."

"He's not saying much yet. He's still poorly, you know. But he said his name was O'Connor. And I suppose I can tell you one of Allen Rienzi's men came in to say there's an American missing from his hotel on Trinidad. Redd O'Connor."

"Has he said what happened to him?"

"Not really," the doctor replied. "He talked about going overboard from a boat. That's all I need to treat him. Anything else can wait for Allen Rienzi."

"Sorry to press you but this is very important," Brett said. "What does he do? Has he said what his job is?"

The consultant's face creased. Plainly, he wanted to get rid of the English police officers and get on with his appointments. He was tempted to say no so that he could escape from them quickly but he did not want to lie. "Allen's colleague found out. He's a private detective."

Brett's eyebrows rose. "Did he say—?"

The doctor interrupted. Walking away backwards, he said, "I have patients to see, Mr Lawless." He turned and strode down the corridor.

"You know," Brett grumbled to Clare, "sometimes I feel frustrated by being a member of the public."

She laughed. "Let's go and do what members of the public do."

Brett sat by the jetty, brushed the grass with his hand and watched it turn brown. Up above them in the hotel's grounds, work on the tennis court wasn't progressing. Earlier in the day, it had been too hot for physical work. In the late afternoon, the workers had managed half an hour of hard labour before it had become too dark to paint along a straight line. Besides, by then, the bars were open.

Clare said, "Who wants to play tennis anyway in this weather?"

Allen appeared beside them and answered, "No one in their right mind. Just the American fitness freaks." He sat down on the grass, causing a considerable patch to play dead.

Clare edged away from Brett slightly. "You look … weary, Allen," she noted. Until that moment, she had not seen him put in enough effort to get tired.

He nodded. "Uh-huh. Your British pace is catching, man. I've been all over the place."

"Did you find Sonny Bourne?"

"Only his jeep," Allen replied, "abandoned on a track in the rainforest. I've been out by car to take a look. It's been there for some time. There's no sign of Sonny himself. He could be anywhere in the forest."

"How do you search it?"

While Allen laughed, a waitress arrived with a tray and three cold Caribs. Obviously, he had ordered them as he passed the bar. Allen handed round the beers and thanked the barmaid. "Search the rainforest? You don't. It's not like a row of houses, you know. Apart from the paths, it's pretty hard to move around in. Most likely Sonny's gone off track and we won't see him again till he comes out."

"How about dogs?"

"Dogs? Plural?" Allen shook his head. "We've got a few dogs trained to sniff things out. All but one are on drugs. The other'll be in the forest at first light. But how many smells are there in a rainforest? Tracking a man among that lot would take a pack of super-hounds. No chance." He drank half of his beer in a single draught.

"Any news from the interviews with Lipner's workers?"

"Nope." Allen reported that all of the Xenox Tobago team had denied knowing about the thiopentone. "And none of them said they'd isolated ricin from castor bean seeds, though they all

141

admitted they had the expertise to do it in that lab of theirs." He shrugged. "But, so what? I know folk in Speyside who can brew up all sorts of things. They can give you powder for cancer, headaches, a sagging love life, a little something to keep your enemies at bay, a broken heart. Whatever. They've got more faith in that than in doctors. And it's all there for free in the rainforest. All you need is the knowledge."

"And your floater?"

Allen smiled. "A friend of mine told me you've already been to the hospital. You know he's Redd O'Connor, private detective."

"Another friend," Brett observed.

"I don't know any more about O'Connor than you yet. I'll visit the hospital tomorrow."

Teasing him, Clare said, "The British pace isn't *that* catching, then. You're not tempted to go now?"

"Tempted, yes," Allen responded with a smile. "But I can resist the temptation till tomorrow. Besides, I've got band practice tonight." He took another drink before saying, "While I'm at the hospital, I've got a job for you."

"Oh?" they both prompted.

"Check out boats in the vicinity of O'Connor's plunge. Dominic Harper's yacht. Fat Maurice. I suppose I've got to include Lee Teshier. And…" He gave a scribbled note to Clare. "Plenty of others. You could have a word with some of them. Like Fat Maurice's customers, especially an English family staying at Crown Point Hotel."

It felt good to be trusted and wanted. At once, they agreed to tackle the job.

They found the British family, the Gormans, in their hotel. The parents were sitting on the balcony of their room, watching their children playing in the gardens below, still deciding what to do with their day. "We've been let down," Mr Gorman complained. "We'd signed up for a trip to the rain-forest today but our rep's just told us the guide's gone missing."

Defending Sonny Bourne, Clare said, "It's true. The police are very concerned about him so it *is* serious. You're not losing your tour for something trivial."

"But we've still lost it," Mrs Gorman replied. "Don't get me wrong, though. I hope the guide's all right."

Brett was examining the large pile of CDs on the dressing table when Mr Gorman commented, "Strange to have English police here. You're nothing to do with Customs, are you?"

Brett smiled. "No. But did you get these CDs from a tall beach trader? Talks from the side of his mouth somehow."

Mr Gorman nodded. "Amazing prices. Much better than at home."

"Yes. Anyway, that's not why we're here. Nothing to do with Customs. We're interested in some events at Buccoo Reef. We understand you went on Fat

Maurice's reef trip on Monday. Is that right?"

"Sheer heaven," Mrs Gorman murmured. "So good, it was our second time."

"Did anything unusual happen?" asked Clare.

"Unusual?"

"Any accidents, fights, arguments?"

"Not really," Mr Gorman answered. "Maurice's helper on the trip got carried away with the rum and got rather drunk. High spirits, that's all."

Mrs Gorman added, "I'll tell you something. It's probably nothing, but... Anyway, when we stopped at the Nylon Pool, I went in swimming first. I saw a red stain on the outside of the boat. Nothing big but it looked like blood."

Brett and Clare both thought of Redd O'Connor's head wound. There was always a lot of blood from injuries to the scalp.

"Did you say anything about it to Fat Maurice?"

She shook her head. "When he noticed me looking at the side of the boat, he got curious. He jumped in and wiped it off with seawater. He said something about going fishing and hauling out a fish. Hooked fish bleed, don't they? I didn't think any more about it."

"Which boat was this?" Brett queried. "He's got several."

Mr Gorman shrugged. "I didn't see the name but it was bright yellow. Very distinctive."

"You said you took two trips. Both with Fat Maurice?" Clare enquired.

"We went almost as soon as we got here as well. Week last Saturday."

"The ninth?"

"Yes," Mr Gorman replied.

It was two days after Ellis McBurnie's murder. Clare asked, "And did anything out of the ordinary happen on that occasion?"

"Well," Mrs Gorman said, "I don't like to mention it. The trip's so good and Maurice is such fun."

"But?"

"A syringe rolled out from under the bench. You never know what you can catch from a needle these days if someone had scratched themselves on it."

"What happened to it?" Clare enquired eagerly.

"As soon as Maurice saw it, he picked it up and threw it overboard. He looked embarrassed and annoyed."

"Anything else worth mentioning?"

"Yes," Mrs Gorman replied. "We all had a great time. The reef ... oh ... absolutely stunning."

Brett and Clare had two new pieces of evidence that could implicate the reef guide in McBurnie's murder and in the attempted murder of O'Connor. Fat Maurice had disposed of a syringe a couple of days after Ellis McBurnie had been injected with a drug and the guide had a blood stain on his boat on the day that Redd O'Connor had fallen into the sea with a head wound. If the investigation had been their own, Brett and Clare would have been on their way to interview Maurice immediately. But because they were assisting Allen, they decided to consult him first.

"Besides," Brett said, "I still don't understand Maurice's motive. And what's the connection between McBurnie and O'Connor?"

Clare could only shrug.

Instead of questioning Fat Maurice, they drove out to Dominic Harper's chateau where they were kept waiting in the reception room for fifteen minutes before Harper entered, sucking on an outsize cigar, and greeted Clare, "Ah, my favourite police officer! How are you getting on, my dear?"

She ignored his disagreeable familiarity and asked who had been on board his yacht and where it was going on the previous Monday.

"Just what *are* you investigating? Last time, you hedged it. You only said it was a serious crime."

"You just haven't got the hang of interviews with a police officer, have you?" Clare snapped impatiently. "I ask a question and you answer it. That's all there is to it. Easy enough. And, by the way, it's become a *very* serious crime so I'd advise you to tell me what your yacht was doing on Monday morning."

Mr Harper was taken aback by her reprimand. A man in his position probably wasn't used to being rebuked. "If you must know," he said, "I went to Port-of-Spain with a couple of hands to pick up a computer, two new DAT master tape decks and other recording equipment."

"Couldn't you have had them delivered?"

Harper laughed. "Obviously you don't know the local couriers. They don't appreciate the meaning of fragile."

"OK. Did you come back with the same number of people that you went with?"

"What's that meant to imply? Of course I did. Talk to them if you want." Between drags on the cigar, Dominic dictated the names and addresses of his crew.

Clare asked, "Did you see anything unusual as you left Tobago waters?"

"Like?"

"Like someone going overboard."

Harper shook his head vehemently. He spoke as if he were explaining a simple idea to a dim and inattentive child. "Obviously not. If we did, we'd go to help. That's what we do round these parts. It's known as the friendly isle."

"A final point," Clare said. "Thursday the seventh of August. You were out yachting with your wife. Did you see your brother-in-law's boat?"

"Haseley? As a matter of fact, we did. I'm not sure he saw us but I picked out his yacht with binoculars. He's a sly one, slipping away from work again."

"Thank you, Mr Harper," Clare replied. "That's all we need for the moment."

Dominic smirked slyly. "Hey, I do a lot for this island. As outsiders, you may not know that. But I do and I'm valued. As a result, I got friends in high places, like Haseley."

Clare shrugged. Unimpressed, she retorted, "We'll bear it in mind."

"I don't think you're taking this matter seriously enough, my dear. I'm trying to be patient with you but, sooner or later, my patience will run out and my friends'll get to hear from me. They wouldn't want anyone to hassle me – or my legitimate business activities – because of the effect it might have on the island's economy."

"We'll worry about the economy," Clare replied, "once we've sorted out truth and justice."

Walking down the plush drive, Brett said, "I think you ruffled a few feathers there. Well done."

Clare murmured, "Prats who call me 'my dear' deserve it."

Brett glanced fondly at his partner and smiled. He admired her more with every moment that he spent with her.

15

Before they met Allen for lunch at Miss Jean's, Brett and Clare fitted in some interviews with other people on Allen's list. The ferry master had not been notified of any trouble on Monday's passage from Trinidad to Tobago. A pair of English tourists who went to Buccoo Reef with Fat Maurice that day did not spot anything out of the ordinary. They were probably too occupied with the scenery to notice any blood stains on the boat. A German visitor who had hired a local man to take him fishing on Monday saw plenty of barracuda but didn't see a human being in the sea. No one could shed any light on the near-drowning of Redd O'Connor.

No one but Redd O'Connor himself.

Allen chewed on Miss Jean's roti and talked at the same time. "He's a colourful character, this Redd

O'Connor." He laughed at his own joke and took another drink of beer.

Keen to hear Allen's report, Brett prompted, "How come he ended up floating offshore?"

"He doesn't know. One moment he's on a job, taking a sneaky look at the recording studio in town on Sunday night. He hears someone behind him and the next thing, he's in hospital with a bump on the head and seaweed in his trousers."

"If he's a private detective, presumably he was on a job."

"Working for IFPI."

"IFPI?"

"International Federation of the Phonographic Industry. The music industry to you and me," Allen explained. "The one that loses ten billion US dollars a year to an illegal trade in pirated tapes and CDs."

"O'Connor was on the trail of pirated CDs?"

"Uh-huh. It's big business, you know. Before coming to meet you, I called a specialist cop in Trinidad. A friend of mine. He said one in every three CDs sold is an illegal copy: a bootleg. That's a lot of sales and royalties – a lot of cash – going to crooks, not the musicians or the proper record label, man. Speaking as a musician, that's not cool."

"So, O'Connor reckoned Dominic Harper's outfit is pirating tapes and CDs?"

"Sounds that way. He was following a lead. That's all he'd say."

"Is he getting out of hospital soon?"

"They're keeping him in a couple of days for observation."

Brett sighed. "Has this CD racket got anything at all to do with Ellis McBurnie?"

Clare said, "You know, we've been stuck in a rut. We've been assuming Ellis died because of the sea slug harvest but maybe we've been barking up the wrong tree. Or snorkelling in the wrong ocean. Everywhere you look into this case, you see CDs. Ellis and Umilta had a big collection, Fat Maurice plays them on No Man's Land, the Gormans are taking a pile home, Dominic Harper makes them, Wilton Cipriani sells them, Redd O'Connor investigates them."

"And what about Isabella McShine?" Brett responded. "I can't see a ninety-two-year-old shaking her pants to American rock."

"Mmm. You've got a point there," Clare admitted. "But take your pick. Either the sea slug's the motive – meaning Redd O'Connor's got nothing to do with it – or pirate CDs are the number-one motive and Isabella McShine's probably got nothing to do with it. Whichever way you jump, one person doesn't fit."

"Or we haven't got a handle on the real motive yet," Allen interjected.

"Don't forget Ellis McBurnie and Isabella McShine had something in common," Brett pointed out. "They were both poisoned with drugs. Suggests the same killer. Anyway, do you know what I think we ought to do next?"

"I guess you're going to tell me," Allen replied.

"We send Forensics to Fat Maurice's yellow boat. Impound it if necessary. See if they can detect traces of blood and, if they do, find out if it's fish or human. And if it's human, whose it is. We need officers to speak to Dominic Harper's crew on the *Katarina*. Do they agree that nothing happened on their Monday trip to Trinidad? That's really important now we know Redd O'Connor was looking into Harper's business. Perhaps Harper's men caught him in the recording studio, cracked him over the head, then took him to the yacht for disposal at sea the next morning. So, when your forensic blood hounds have finished with Fat Maurice, they should check the sound studio and the *Katarina* for signs of O'Connor. Blood, hair, any other traces."

"Take it easy, man. That's enough for our forensic department to be getting on with. We haven't got whole teams of scientists, you know. This is Tobago, not England." Allen looked at Clare and said, "Is he always like this? There's a hint of a lead and he sends in an army of gurus."

Clare smiled and nodded. "That's our Brett." She touched her partner's arm and said, "But, to be fair, he gets results."

"All right, I'll get Forensics on the job," Allen said. "*And* we'll do some talking. I want to hear if Fat Maurice has got a different explanation for the blood and the hypo. I'll put a couple of officers on to the *Katarina* crew. There's Dominic Harper and the recording studio as well. They're used to me down there so I'll talk to them and take a look around – like I'm thinking of my next recording session. And I'll tackle Wilton because he's my mate. I'll see if he knows anything dodgy about Harper's tapes and CDs." Allen took off his sunglasses and wiped his brow. "So, it looks like you two get Fat Maurice."

"And Umilta McBurnie," Clare said. "We need a quick word about her CD collection."

Allen looked troubled at the mention of the powerful politician's lover but he didn't try to stop them. He nodded briefly and replaced his sunglasses, hiding his eyes. "Who'll you do first? On Wednesdays, Maurice usually gives himself a day off the trip and stays in his tour office."

Brett shrugged. "The order doesn't matter. Probably Maurice."

Allen nodded his approval and then said, "You know, I bumped into Haseley Abidh at the hospital."

"He wasn't paying Redd O'Connor a visit, was he?" Brett asked urgently. He was aware that O'Connor's would-be killer could turn up at the hospital to finish a bungled job.

Allen shook his head. "Apparently his mother's been very ill. A surgeon friend told me. She's recovering from cancer. Nothing to do with this case."

"How about your CD specialist friend from Trinidad?" Brett queried. "Can he come over and take a look at Dominic Harper's set-up?"

"He's on his way – as soon as he can get some time and a plane seat," Allen answered.

"Any news of Sonny Bourne?"

Allen shook his head, genuinely concerned. He finished the dregs of his mercifully cold beer. Perking up, he said, "See you guys this evening at Turtle Beach Hotel for an update."

"Ah, yes," Brett said happily. "Your Wednesday gig."

Allen stood up. "Uh–huh. Bring your dancing shoes. I feel a good one coming on." He gyrated his hips, clapped his hands and boomed, "Yeah." He walked away with a more purposeful stride than normal.

When the British detectives consulted the map they changed their minds. It was more convenient to make Umilta McBurnie their first port of call. While they waited for her to answer their knock on the front door, there was the unmistakable sound of another door opening and closing hurriedly at the rear of the house. Clare and Brett looked at each other and shared a frown. "You stay here," Clare said quickly. "I'll go and take a peek."

Brett nodded and Clare dashed round the corner out of sight.

At the side of the house there was a wild garden. Bushes with white and pink flowers, a palm tree that looked like a giant unfolded fan, and plants with large yellow blooms. Clare picked her way through the exotic flora to reach the back of Umilta's property. The secluded garden was bounded by trees. Two white plastic chairs were positioned under a thatched umbrella but they were empty. A rough track led down towards the ocean and a small jetty where, Clare assumed, Ellis had moored his launch until the police had impounded it. Now, a man was bending down, untying the rope that held a small motorboat to the private pier. He had his back to her.

Taking a deep breath, Clare began to sprint down the long track. She knew that she did not stand a chance of reaching the boat before it sped away but she hoped she'd get close enough to recognize Umilta's guest who was in such a hurry to leave. Clare put out her left hand to sweep to one side the fronds of a tree that encroached across the path. The track was so rough that she could not keep her eyes on the man at the waterside. She had to watch where she was planting her feet. When she could look up, she saw that he was wearing light trousers and a green shirt. A large white hat protected the back of his head and neck. She sprinted as quickly as she could but the man jumped into his boat, started it and in one practised manoeuvre, accelerated away from the jetty.

Clare cursed and came to a halt, still several metres short of the mooring point. She held a hand to her brow and squinted out to sea. Even though she was wearing shades, the sun reflected off the ocean and shone in her eyes like a blinding headlight. She could not read any markings on the back of the speedboat and she could not distinguish the man himself. She shook her head in annoyance. She had not even been able to decide if he was black or white, young or old, bald or long-haired. She knew only that it was a man and he used a motorboat. On Tobago, that would describe half of the population.

She turned and walked back up to the house. When she joined Brett in Umilta's air-conditioned lounge, her subtle expression told her partner that she'd spotted the secret guest but had failed to identify him. Clare looked directly into Umilta's face and asked, "When he visits you, does he always come by boat?"

Umilta frowned. "Who?" She wasn't going to be tricked into giving a name without first finding out what the English policewoman had seen.

Clare nodded towards the back of the house. "You know who. Your visitor."

Umilta gazed coolly into Clare's face. "Obviously it would be wrong, so soon after Ellis's death, to ... you know. So Haseley tends to be prudent when he comes here. I'm sure you understand. For the sake of my reputation and his career, he does not wish to be seen."

"Yes," Clare said. "I understand."

Sensing that Clare would not be able to push that line of inquiry any further, Brett reminded Umilta, "You were telling me where your music CDs came from."

"Yes. I was explaining that I used to buy them

from a shop in town but I came to an arrangement with a man called Wilton Cipriani. He got them direct from Mr Harper so he could make a substantial saving. There was no shop to take a percentage of the profit. Even then, they were very cheap. Very good value."

"Weren't you suspicious of them?"

"I thought that you were helping to look into my husband's death."

Brett answered, "We are. Did Ellis have anything to do with this trade in CDs?"

"Certainly not. If something did not live underwater, he soon lost interest." There was considerable resentment in her tone.

"And do you think the CDs are perfectly legitimate?" Brett asked.

Umilta smiled wryly. "I would be surprised if they were. I like to think that I'm a shrewd businesswoman who can recognize a scam when she sees one. I expect they are copies of the real thing. Very good copies. Of course, I would claim that I bought them in good faith."

"Of course," Brett echoed.

Back in the car, Brett asked, "Well? Was it Haseley who shot out the back door?"

Clare shrugged helplessly. "It could have been Big John Macfarlane for all I know, Brett. Sorry."

Brett chuckled softly at the notion.

"On second thoughts," Clare said, "perhaps not. It was only a small boat he got away in."

*   *   *

The office of Fat Maurice Tours was a tip. Hardly enough room for the big man himself and a telephone for taking bookings. Brett and Clare squeezed into the remaining space and listened to Fat Maurice's frosty denial.

"Blood stain?" He shook his head and his several chins wobbled at once. "A bit too much rum I think your tourist had." Then he laughed and added, "A rum and Coke stain more likely."

"Apparently you jumped into the water and washed it off."

"Did I? You might be right. I can't remember."

"You also said it was from a fish you'd caught."

"Could be. But whatever it was, I wouldn't want it on my boat so, yeah, I'm sure I'd wash it off." He dabbed his forehead with a handkerchief and then shuffled scraps of paper on the desk.

"There was something else. On Saturday the ninth."

"Ancient history," Fat Maurice groaned, waving away the notion with his hand and accidentally dropping the hankie. "Today and tomorrow are all I've got time for. Life's too short to look back. Live for today, plan for the next day and that's it."

"Even so, I need to ask you about ancient history because that's when Ellis McBurnie died. I understand a hypodermic syringe turned up on your boat that Saturday."

"More rumours from tourists?"

"Sober ones," Brett stressed.

Wheezing, Fat Maurice reached down to pick up his handkerchief. When he straightened up, he did not dispute the find. "Yeah. I remember. I *did* find a syringe and I wasn't amused. It was nothing to do with me. Believe me, I don't want to get a bad reputation and I don't want to get closed down. I imagine one of the tourists brought it onboard, taking advantage of my hospitality. I don't know who. Obviously they thought they could bring their nasty drug habits with them – to make the trip go with an even bigger swing. As if the scenery and what I provide isn't enough." He sighed loudly. "Pathetic."

"That's your explanation, is it?" Brett responded.

"What else do you want? A fairy story?"

"You play a few CDs on the beach at No Man's Land," Clare observed. "Where did they come from?"

"Come from? How do you mean?"

"Where did you buy them?"

Maurice smiled at her. "The music shop in town. And the tapes are direct from Allen Rienzi. His band's not bad, you know."

Clare nodded. "We've heard them. Very good."

The telephone rang and, while Fat Maurice listened to his caller, he kept glancing at Brett and Clare. "Are they really?" he said into the mouthpiece. "Yeah, well, you'll have to co-operate with them. Yep. Co-operate. Blood stains are what they're looking for, if I'm not mistaken. I've got those British cops with me now. I dare say they're behind it. Yep. No problem. Thanks for letting me know." He put the phone down and said, "Some forensic people are going over one of my boats. Your idea?"

"We don't have any power to order anything here on Tobago but," Brett admitted, "yes, the police thought it was a good idea to check."

Fat Maurice let out a long breath. "Well, for what it's worth, I'm co-operating. You heard me."

Brett nodded. "Thanks. We'll leave you in peace for now."

Strolling back to the car, Clare remarked, "He's hiding something."

"He was lying, you reckon?"

"His body language was all over the place. He wasn't comfortable. There was certainly a bit of fibbing going on in there. Minimum."

Brett was inclined to trust his partner's instinct. "We'll be in a better position to push him on that once Forensic's done its stuff on the boat." He took a step forward and stopped in Clare's path. "Clare," he said, bringing her to a halt, "I want to test something out on you."

"Oh?"

"It's Allen Rienzi. I don't know. I have my worries about him, I suppose."

16

"Allen's a good guy," Brett said. "A bit secretive – obstructive – at first, but you thought that was perfectly natural. I agree. But we don't really know him, do we?"

"What are you saying, Brett?" Clare asked.

Perched overhead on a telephone wire, some small scarlet-breasted soldier birds suddenly let out excited and disproportionate calls. Each of them emitted a short *chip* and then a long wheezing note.

"He admits he likes Umilta McBurnie. That man you ran after at her place, could it have been Allen?"

"It *could* have, yes. The build and trousers were about right but at lunch he was in a T-shirt. If it was Allen, he must've slipped into a green shirt since then."

"He asked who we were going to see first. Fat

Maurice, we said. Perhaps he thought he'd got the time to pay Umilta a quick visit and warn her we were on our way. But then we switched the order."

Clare shook her head dismissively. "Falling for Umilta – maybe. But murder her husband? Not our Allen." She glanced at her watch. "We're OK for time. I think this conversation's going to need a beer back at the hotel."

Brett smiled and agreed.

Sitting by the pool at Tropikist, they sipped cold drinks. Brett sat out in the sunshine, prodding the changeable grass with his feet, while Clare remained under the shade of the parasol. "OK," she said. "Run your theory past me."

"I'm not sure it's a theory about the murders. Just an uneasiness about motives. Allen didn't exactly rush to get us an interview with Umilta McBurnie and when he did, he hardly said a word but she looked to him quite a lot."

"In case you hadn't noticed, Allen doesn't rush to do anything," Clare replied. "Besides, if you're implying Allen and Umilta are a couple, what's this about Haseley Abidh?"

"That's the bit that's worrying me. Put yourself in her place. What if she's got a lover? Allen, say. She's desperate to be free of Ellis but doesn't want to kill him herself. She'd be an obvious suspect. She'd want to keep her distance from the actual murder. She doesn't want her lover to do it either. If he did, he might get caught and then they'd be separated. That defeats the object." Brett took a drink and, for a second, watched a brown pelican plummeting into the sea. "So, what does she do? She's an attractive woman. She uses her feminine charms on Haseley Abidh and pretends to fall for him. She says she wants to marry him and gets him to remove hubby. She doesn't care if Abidh gets done for murder. If he gets caught and tries to drag her down with him, she just denies having anything to do with it. She'd say he was so besotted with her that he killed Ellis on his own. There'd be no evidence against her. Just the word of a murderer against a good-looking widow. No contest."

"If you're right, why pick such a high-profile chap?"

"*Because* he's high profile. She's thinking through every eventuality. If he does the murder and actually gets away with it, Umilta would have to have a plan to leave him and take up with her real lover. A politician protecting his position isn't likely to get his own back on her for desertion by shopping her. His career wouldn't survive the scandal. A lesser mortal might not be so bothered abut wrecking his own life and might come clean about the whole thing."

"That's ... devious," Clare said. "And far-fetched."

"But possible."

"Sure. With anyone taking the role of Umilta's real lover, not just Allen," she said, keeping her voice down. She knew that Allen Rienzi had friends everywhere. "But, tell me, why was Umilta so slow to point the finger at Abidh if he's the fall guy?"

"Because she's acting. Playing the part of Abidh's lover. If she spilled the beans straight away, we'd be suspicious, wouldn't we? We'd be asking ourselves why she gave way so easily. Remember, though, Allen already knew about Haseley Abidh. That fits if he was in on the plan."

Clare exhaled loudly. "I can't believe it of Allen. What's wrong with the obvious? Jason Lipner got rid of the opposition on the reef — with or without the help of Lee Teshier — and then removed Isabella McShine and Sonny Bourne so his alibi couldn't be refuted. Redd O'Connor doesn't fit because that's a separate case. The case of the fraudulent CDs."

"I agree," Brett stressed. "That's the number-one possibility. The simplest comes first. The big pharmaceutical business flexing its muscles. The second's something to do with the big bootleg business and it involves Redd O'Connor. But there's no harm having a third idea waiting in the wings."

"How would Isabella McShine and Sonny Bourne fit into your love triangle theory, anyway?"

Brett replied, "That's the clever bit."

"Oh, no. Not another little complication!" With an impudent grin, she said, "Your brain's been affected by the heat. Sunstroke."

Brett laughed. "Imagination working overtime," he admitted. "No doubt Haseley Abidh's a clever chap. If Umilta persuaded him to murder her husband, he'd sort out an alibi, wouldn't he? Years ago, he knew Sonny Bourne. To be confirmed, but it's likely. Through Sonny, he knew about Isabella and ricin. Through his job in the Trade Department, he knew about Lipner. All the ingredients are there. He just needs a recipe. He decides to frame Jason Lipner. Right? He gets Sonny Bourne to arrange a meeting between Lipner and Mrs McShine at the time when he's off murdering Ellis McBurnie. Afterwards, he kills Isabella and disappears Sonny, leaving Lipner with an alibi that can't be checked. He also got Umilta to go with him in his yacht so they could give each other alibis."

"Ruining her plan to keep her distance from the murder."

Brett frowned and hesitated, trying to work out where his ideas were taking him. "Not quite," he said. "She would've gone along with Abidh's plan because, if she'd refused, she'd have raised his suspicions. More or less forced to go. But she'd still want to protect herself. So," he suggested, "Umilta offered to sail the yacht north while Abidh took off to Buccoo in another boat. That way, she *did* keep her distance and gave Abidh the alibi he wanted."

Clare nodded. "I see what you're getting at. That's why their yacht was a long way from Buccoo Reef. Neat. Ingenious, in fact." She hesitated, thinking, before continuing, "But if it is Abidh and he knew all about ricin, why did he bother with a barbiturate to kill Ellis? Why didn't he just use ricin? It's a bit of a roundabout method."

"Yeah. But ricin doesn't leave a trace. Good for Isabella because he was going for natural causes. But he'd *want* the drug found in McBurnie — to incriminate anyone at Xenox. That's why he used thiopentone."

"There's still a problem," Clare pointed out. "A big one. How come a government trade minister with a background in business studies knows enough about thiopentone to murder McBurnie with it?"

"I didn't say it was a perfect picture. Otherwise it'd be up at number one."

At Turtle Beach Hotel, Brett and Clare updated Allen on their interviews with Umilta McBurnie and Fat Maurice. Then Allen reported on progress with Dominic Harper. "He said his biggest problem was drunken musicians breaking his recording equipment. I can believe that." He laughed at a private memory of mayhem inspired by calypso and Caribs. "Harper denied having anything to do with pirated cassettes and CDs. But," Allen added, "he would, wouldn't he?"

"The *Katarina* crew?" Brett prompted.

"Well drilled. According to them, the journey was all plain sailing," Allen said. "I didn't believe a word. I think they dumped O'Connor."

"If they did, your forensic people should confirm it. If he was on the boat he'll have left traces. Fibres, hair, blood."

Two young women strutted past them and chimed, "Hi, Allen."

Allen replied, "How you doing, girls? Hot one tonight." He looked towards the stage. "Time I was setting up with the band."

"What about Wilton Cipriani?" Clare asked.

Allen smiled. "I know him. No problem. He's my friend, man. His mouth said one thing and his eyes said another. He doesn't want to lose the work Harper puts his way so he wouldn't testify to anything but he knows the tapes and CDs aren't what they should be. And before now he's loaded up the *Katarina* with CDs that have come from our studio even though the music's by groups that have never set foot on Tobago. Redd O'Connor had his nose on the right scent." He stood up and declared, "Anyway, don't talk to me about work. I'm off duty. Are you guys staying for the show?"

"Of course," Clare replied. "We'll be your litmus test. If you can get us on our feet again, you must be doing good."

As he walked away, Allen said, "It's a deal. I accept the challenge." Since lunch, he had changed. He now wore a brilliant green silk shirt.

The black silhouettes of palm trees stood out against the orange afterglow of the sun and a hearty breeze swept away the heat of day. A few wispy clouds smudged the vivid sky. The music was as riotous and irresistible as it had been at Crown Point. After a few cocktails, Brett and Clare were cavorting like a couple of enthusiastic kids, revelling in the rhythms, the atmosphere, revelling in each other. Murder was a million miles away. Crime was inconceivable. And Allen was just a musician.

Clare stopped dancing, moved behind Brett and held him by his shoulders. Pointing him at Allen, she said into his ear, "Listen to him, Brett. That's not someone who participates in some wild murder scheme. Music and murder don't mix, man. Despite the shirt. It's just not possible."

After a while, Brett turned and said, "OK. It's unlikely, I'll give you that. But…"

Clare shook her head at his obstinacy.

When the steel band had finished for the evening, Brett and Clare took a stroll along the beach. The hotel lamps and the moon gave out just enough light to see the seashore. The night was utterly tranquil. As they walked with the wind at their backs, their hands touched occasionally. "You know," Brett breathed, "it seems like an eternity but it was only four weeks ago when my mate Phil said we made a natural pair."

"A natural pair? He was probably talking about us being partners in crime."

"I tried to misunderstand him as well. I talked – you'd call it preaching – about how we need to value each other as professionals, not on a personal level. But no. He meant, we make a good couple." Brett smiled at the memory. "Young Kerry called you my girlfriend and told me to be careful because she said you're dangerous as well as attractive." His hand squeezed hers.

The murmur from the hotel had subsided. The only noises came from the wind and the waves nuzzling the beach.

"Attractive and dangerous, eh? Like the sea." Clare halted. "I bet John Macfarlane would say it's naughty to take a dip together right now."

Brett laughed. "No doubt about it."

"So?"

Brett looked at their flimsy clothes and said, "What the hell. Let's go." He propelled her into the warm water. Buffeted by the waves, they swam out a little way into the Caribbean Sea and then turned parallel to the shore. "Swim back towards the hotel?"

"Good idea."

Side by side, they swam a leisurely breaststroke until they neared Turtle Beach Hotel. Treading water, Brett said, "That was great. Crazy as well." He hesitated and then added, "Did I ever tell you? You make a terrific partner."

"You're not so bad yourself," Clare replied. "Good dancer, powerful swimmer, so-so detective." Then she let out a quiet cry of shock and spun round.

"What's up?" Brett asked her.

"Something just touched me on the back. But I can't see anything."

"Seaweed?"

"No. Quite solid."

Suddenly concerned for her, Brett asked, "It wasn't sharp, was it?"

"No," she answered. "More like a thump than a stab. No harm done."

Brett was relieved. "Probably a fish or turtle. Lots of them here. Perfectly harmless. Perhaps it was curious, hungry or short-sighted."

"Yeah. Unnerving in the dark, though. Scarier than your spider. Let's get out. Just in case there's sharks."

They dragged themselves out on to the beach where the tropical wind began immediately to dry them. Brett lifted up a hand, about to brush back the wet hairs from Clare's face, when he hesitated, embarrassed.

Clare smiled mischievously. "It's all right, Detective Inspector Lawless. I'm not one of those female spiders that eats the male after she's had her bit of fun. Not a black widow. No matter what you've heard about me. I'm not *that* dangerous."

"Sure?"

"Certain."

They hugged each other and kissed. Imitating Allen, Brett said, "Relax."

"Enjoy," Clare responded immediately.

Usually, when Brett was on a case, time rushed past in a blur. He was so focused on the investigation that a normal life passed him by. He was blinkered by the need for an arrest. Now, holding a sopping wet woman, time seemed to slow down. The busy pace of life dropped to a blissful zero. He had not experienced that luxurious suspension from the real world for a very long time. It felt like effortless floating. And he was pleased that it was Clare who shared the moment with him. Dripping on the sand, he did not even feel daft. Or, if they were being daft, he didn't care.

"All right?" he whispered.

Clare nodded. "A gal could do a lot worse."

"A walk to the car to dry off and then back home?"

"Home?" Clare said. "You *are* getting used to Tobago, aren't you?"

"Sheffield has its attractions but this is ... very special."

The British advisers had finally adopted Allen's unhurried approach to the case. In the morning, they woke themselves up with a few lazy lengths of the pool and then they loitered over the fresh fruit and coffee at breakfast. Above them, there was a rumble and then the growl of jet engines bringing the usual morning delivery of European tourists. Brett and Clare talked about past romances, laughing over the disasters that seemed so awful at the time, about music, tropical fish, art and Clare's favourite poetry. Eventually, though, murder had to encroach on their idyll.

On the way to the police headquarters in Scarborough, they stopped at the harbour and examined Abidh's yacht. By some standards, it was a modest vessel but it still looked posh to Brett and

Clare. At its stern, a motorized dinghy was tied. Presumably it was towed as a lifeboat in case of emergency. "There you are," Brett said. "Abidh could've set out with Umilta in the yacht and one of them could have shot off to Buccoo in the motorboat."

Clare nodded. "Sometime, we should pressure Umilta on that. After all, if she's behind her husband's death and she's using Abidh as a scapegoat, she might sacrifice him if we squeeze her."

"For now, Allen needs to put an officer on surveillance outside her house. It'd be fascinating to see who her callers are."

The tethered boats were bobbing about on the water more than normal. The wind had died down but there was a considerable swell, the strongest that the English detectives had seen since their arrival in the West Indies. Away from the harbour, the sea was choppy.

With her forefinger, Clare traced the faint line of blue marks down Brett's right forearm. "Nearly gone," she observed.

"That's modern antibiotics – and a strong constitution – for you."

In the police station, Allen and his friend from Trinidad were supposed to be scrutinizing a large pile of tapes and CDs that Allen had confiscated from Wilton. Instead, the two friends looked as if they were simply enjoying listening to the music on one of the cassette players that was usually reserved for recording interviews. When Brett and Clare entered the room, Allen stopped drumming a beat with his hands on the table, switched off the tape and said, "We've got a verdict, man." He waved an arm at the chaotic stack of cassettes and compact discs. "They're all forgeries."

The specialist added, "The packaging artwork's not up to scratch – poor quality colour photocopying – and some of the designs printed on the CDs themselves are below par. I've seen better bootlegs and I've seen a lot worse."

Allen said, "We'll set up a raid later today. Harper's the main target and his workers are in trouble, including Wilton, I'm afraid."

"You got the forensic results, then," Brett guessed.

"We got O'Connor's hair and blood on board the *Katarina*, as well as a trace of his blood between the cracks of the sound studio floor. But," Allen said, "I also need to have a chat with Fat Maurice before he goes off on a reef tour."

"You got results from his boat as well?"

"Tiny amounts of human blood. It's not the same group as Redd O'Connor's, though."

Brett enquired, "Ellis McBurnie?"

"Nope. Not his either," Allen answered. "No idea whose. Anyway, he'll talk to me, maybe. You white folk don't speak his sort of language." Allen pointed to the tapes and said, "You two guys can unwind. Enjoy the evidence. See you later."

"Before you go, Allen," Brett said, "tell me *where*

you found Lipner's business card in Isabella McShine's place."

Allen flicked through the forensic report, scanning each page with his finger. After a while, he answered, "In the bin, under a chicken carcass."

Suddenly, Brett became very attentive. "Say that again."

"In the bin."

"No. The chicken-bone bit."

"It says here his card was found under a boiled chicken carcass. Why, man?"

"Because it's very important." Brett did not reveal his thoughts. Instead, he asked, "Where was Jason Lipner in the morning and early afternoon of Thursday the seventh?"

"According to witnesses, he was at work. He left at about two o'clock."

"Is that for sure?"

"Uh-huh. Several people said so independently."

"I see." Unexpectedly, Brett announced, "Almost certainly, that's Lipner off the hit list, then."

Allen looked dumbly at Brett and then at Clare.

Clare had read her partner's mind. She was nodding in agreement with his deduction. "You go and get Fat Maurice to talk," she said to Allen. "We couldn't. If I'm not mistaken, we need another chat with Evelyn McShine. Right, Brett?"

"Right. Then," Brett said to Allen, "I'll tell you why Jason Lipner's innocent – despite all the evidence against him."

17

Under the dark roof of broad banana leaves, Brett said to Isabella McShine's daughter, "I'm sorry but there's two more questions we'd like to ask you. Last time, you said your mum enjoyed chicken callaloo most afternoons?"

Evelyn eyed the two detectives and demanded to know, "What's that got to do with anything?" She took a small jar of aromatic leaves from the table and slipped it into her apron pocket, out of sight.

Brett ignored her use of native resources. This time, he wasn't interested in the concoctions that she might prepare for herself, her brother and their circle of friends. "The timing might just clear someone of murder," Brett answered.

"And it might cast some light on your mother's death," Clare added.

"What are you saying? Her death was deliberate? They told me it was natural."

Clare decided that being open with the woman was the only way forward. "That might not be right, I'm afraid."

"And if I answer your questions, you'll tell me what you know?"

"As much as we can, yes," Clare agreed.

Evelyn sighed. "All right. What was it again?"

"When your mother had her callaloo," said Clare.

"A woman of habit, my mam. She had it mid-afternoon every time. About three-thirty."

"OK. When you found her, did you throw the chicken carcass in the bin?"

Evelyn shook her head. "Mam had already done that. She always cleaned up while she waited for the callaloo to cool. That was her routine."

"Are you sure? It's *very* important."

"The chicken bones are important?" Evelyn leaned forward. "You mean it *was* something in the callaloo?"

"No, I don't think so. But that's not what I'm getting at," Clare replied. "Her visitor – the one the police think may have committed a murder at three o'clock that afternoon – his business card was in your mum's bin. She must have put it there. Not interested in the Xenox offer at all. The bones were on top of it. You see, if his card had been on top of the bones, he could've dropped in any time after her afternoon snack. But it was under. She binned the business card *before* the bones so he must have been with her at about three o'clock – or before. But he left Scarborough at two. He couldn't have got to Speyside much sooner."

"You're sure you didn't tip out the chicken bones?" Brett checked.

Evelyn nodded.

"Then our suspect's telling the truth. He *was* at your mum's around three o'clock."

Evelyn said, "But what does all this mean about my mam's death?"

"We don't know for sure," Brett admitted, "but we think someone put ricin from castor bean seeds in something she took later."

"Poisoned!" Evelyn looked startled and suddenly vengeful. "Who? Was it this visitor – the one with the business card?"

Brett shook his head. "I doubt it. He wanted your mum very much alive. He wanted to learn from her. It was probably someone else who didn't want us to prove the Xenox man had been with her."

"Mam died for *that*? She died just so she couldn't say she'd had a visitor?"

Both Brett and Clare nodded sadly. "We think so."

"Then she died for nothing." Evelyn was very angry. "When you find out who it was, you tell me. I'll prepare him a little something."

While Brett retreated, Clare stepped forward and said, "We can't do that. But we're doing our best to catch him. Then it's up to the law."

Evelyn stared into Clare's face for a few seconds

and then murmured, "I believe you." Before Clare could pull away, Evelyn took her elbow in her rough hand and whispered, "He's very fond of you." She nodded at Brett. "If you want to keep him, I can give you something to put into his drink…"

Clare smiled. "No. It's OK, thanks. I don't need… I'll handle whatever happens."

When Jason saw Brett and Clare at his door yet again, he exclaimed, "Give me a break! What have I got to do to convince you?"

"Absolutely nothing, as far as we're concerned," Brett replied. "We're convinced already. Just tell us what *exactly* was Isabella doing when you went to see her?"

Dr Lipner did not perk up after hearing Brett's revelation. Perhaps he suspected that the British police officers were pulling some sort of devious trick. He replied, "She had an apron on. I suppose she was preparing a meal. While we talked, she kept the apron on."

"And what did you suppose she was going to do when you left? Anything?"

"Return to her cooking, I should think."

"Thank you, Dr Lipner," Brett declared. "That all fits. Now, I need to have a word with your colleague who saw a burglar in here late one night."

"That's Crawford. He's in the lab right now."

Brett and Clare were working on the theory that someone had tried to frame Lipner. One part of the phoney case against him was the bottle of thiopentone that had turned up in his laboratory. It was possible that the culprit had got hold of some of the barbiturate, taken what he needed to poison McBurnie, and planted the remainder in the Xenox lab before the killing.

In the aquarium room, Crawford was peering into a tank where two *Dendronotus* were looking decidedly unhappy. They were not going to be alive for long.

To the biologist, Brett said, "According to Dr Lipner, you thought the burglar was Ellis McBurnie, trying to damage the lab or something. But you arrived at work late and scared him off before he could do anything. Did you get a good look at him?"

"Not really. The lights were off when I went into the chemistry lab. He must have been behind the door. As soon as it began to close, before I turned the lights on, he slipped out."

"First, are you sure it was a him, not a her?"

"Definitely a man. He was black, I think, though I couldn't be a hundred per cent sure," Crawford answered.

"Could it have been anyone else you know? Not Ellis McBurnie."

"He was about McBurnie's build. But, yes, it could've been almost anyone. I just assumed it was McBurnie up to no good."

"And he was in the lab where the police found that bottle of thiopentone, wasn't he?" Brett pointed towards the adjoining room.

Crawford nodded. "Yes. The chemistry lab."

When Clare tried to extract a fuller picture of the intruder from Crawford, she had little success. His vague description ruled out only the extremes, like Wilton Cipriani and Fat Maurice, but almost any other reasonably agile black male would have fitted.

The planting of the murder weapon at Xenox remained a fanciful but enticing theory. Brett was left with one vital question that he could not answer. If a pharmaceutical chemist like Lipner wasn't the murderer, who else would know enough about thiopentone?

Confronted with hard evidence, a scared Wilton Cipriani had confessed everything he knew to Allen. He'd testified that, on the Wednesday before McBurnie's murder, the *Katarina* had been in harbour to load up with pirate CDs, copied illegally in the recording studio. They were bound for the lucrative American market. His statement condemned Dominic Harper.

Harper was being held on charges of copyright fraud, malicious assault, and the attempted murder of Redd O'Connor. The two-man crew of the *Katarina*, Harper's henchmen, would be rounded up and charged with aiding and abetting. The case had been concluded. "Nothing to do with Ellis McBurnie and Isabella McShine," Allen said to Brett and Clare. "You helped but it's not why you're here."

"So, the music motive's off the list," Clare

concluded. "That leaves us with a therapeutic sea slug and a little thing called love. Love should be therapeutic as well." She hesitated a moment before asking, "What about Fat Maurice? Any joy?"

"I wouldn't say joy," Allen replied, "but you can forget him. He *was* trying to hide something, for sure, but it's not our patch. He told me all about it. The guy who helps him, the one who looks like he's drunk too much, he's got a more serious problem. It's not just alcohol. He's got a heroin habit. Sometimes he staggers around a bit, sometimes he falls and bangs his head on the side of the boat, sometimes there's a hypo and a bit of blood. Sending in the drug cops isn't going to solve anything for him. Fat Maurice was protecting him but the big man's trying to help him kick the habit as well. The best thing is to leave it with Maurice. A bit of trust and understanding beats heavy-handed law any day."

"Any news of Sonny Bourne?" Clare queried.

Allen merely shook his head and looked away.

"How's Redd O'Connor?"

"No problem. He's coming out of hospital, man, not much the worse for wear."

"Hospital," Brett murmured to himself.

Clare and Allen both looked at him, puzzled.

Brett was nodding. "Yeah. Hospital. That's it! Time to see your surgeon friend, Allen."

The hospital consultant wouldn't answer Brett when he asked about Mrs Abidh's recuperation. He claimed that patient confidentiality would not allow him to discuss it.

In frustration, Brett stressed, "We don't want any details of the patient. Not much, anyway. We already know she's got – or had – cancer. The question is, *how* was she treated?" Stretching the truth a little, he claimed, "It's just a general enquiry about cancer treatment in this hospital. Would you use radio-therapy, an operation, chemotherapy? All three?"

Obstinately, the doctor responded, "We *are* deal-ing with a minister's mother here."

Allen stepped forward with a grin. He flung an arm round his friend and enquired, "How you doing? OK?"

"Not so bad. We could use more money, more equipment, more troops."

Allen threw up his hands. "Tell me about it, man. I'm so short-staffed, I have to import Brits!" He jerked his thumb at Brett and Clare. "Still, got to make the best of it. And we've got to be patient with them – and their peculiar British ways. You see," Allen said, keeping his voice down, "if I'm going to hit this one for six, I *do* need just a touch of info. Nothing that'll land you in trouble. We don't even want to know what sort of cancer or how she's doing. No problem. But it'd help to know if she's had an operation. That's all."

Buttered up by Allen, the surgeon nodded. "Yes, she has. But I didn't tell you that."

"I didn't hear a thing," Allen replied. "I suppose her son's been in a lot?"

"Naturally."

Unable to stay out of it, Brett asked, "And did he take an interest in the details of her operation?" Rapidly, he added, "We're not interested ourselves, you understand. We just want to know if *he* did."

The doctor sighed and looked at Allen. Seeing his friend nod encouragement, he replied, "As a matter of fact, he did, yes."

"Let me guess," Brett said. "He took a particular interest in the anaesthetic." Again the consultant nodded. "And the anaesthetic was?"

"Thiopentone."

Brett smiled, clenched a fist in celebration, and said, "Thank you. That's all we need."

Later, when they checked with the pharmacy, they discovered that the hospital's use of thiopentone and the remaining stock did not account for the total supply. One bottle had gone missing. Brett anticipated that anyone could have walked in surreptitiously at a quiet moment and strolled away with the lost bottle.

That evening, the air became even hotter and stickier than normal. A distant thin haze of cloud gave a dull red sunset. Clare glanced at it affectionately. "*Red sky at night, shepherds' delight.*"

Allen frowned. "I've never heard that one. It's not like that here, man. High pressure, humid, dirty sunset, it all adds up to no good. No delight in that."

Brett was quiet and thoughtful. It was precisely two weeks since Ellis McBurnie's death and he felt that he was near to unravelling the mystery.

On Friday morning, Allen let out a long sigh. The thought of interviewing Haseley Abidh again did not thrill him. But he knew as well as Brett and Clare that it had to be done. The minister was in deep trouble.

On the way to the government building, Clare remarked, "Wind's really getting up."

"What did I tell you last night? Didn't you watch the TV in your room?" Allen replied, looking away from the road for an alarming amount of time. "We're going to catch the edge of Hurricane Hattie. Right now, the pressure's dropping like a ripe coconut, man. Hattie only has to change course a bit and you'll experience one of the less picturesque aspects of Caribbean life. It doesn't happen a lot – we're south of the main hurricane belt – but when it does… A devil let loose in heaven."

Mr Abidh's secretary put up several obstacles to protect her boss from intrusion. "You can't just barge in," she declared. "He's a minister! He's got important business and a very tight schedule."

"Investigating two deaths isn't trivial," Allen said in a tone that was not as assertive as it should have been.

"You can't seriously think Mr Abidh..." the exasperated secretary gasped.

"Look," Brett chipped in. "Officer Rienzi is trying to be diplomatic and sympathetic. I don't have to be. I imagine Mr Abidh would rather help us with our inquiry informally here and now than be escorted to the police station in full view of the public."

The secretary looked into Brett's face and realized that she would not be able to undermine his determination. "Just a minute," she said. "I'll go and have a word."

When they were shepherded into Abidh's office, he was already looking at his watch. "You've got five minutes," he announced curtly.

Unperturbed, Brett shrugged. "That's enough. We're talking to everyone who knows Sonny Bourne. Am I right in thinking you're acquainted with him from your time as manager of a health club?"

"What's the problem?"

"As you haven't given us long, I'd appreciate it if you answer the question."

Cautiously, the politician said, "Yes. He did a bit of work for me."

"Like, provide folk remedies?"

Haseley shrugged, not wanting to commit himself.

"Did he ever tell you about ricin?"

"No," Abdih stated bluntly.

"Castor bean seeds?"

He shook his head.

"Did you visit Umilta McBurnie's house on Wednesday afternoon?" asked Brett.

Haseley frowned for a second. "No."

"Strange. Umilta said you did. That's how she explained the man who ran out of her place when we called." Brett felt justified in sowing the seeds of doubt in the suspect's mind. Before Haseley could respond, Brett posed the key question. "Do you know anything about thiopentone?"

"I've never heard of it."

Brett pounced. Feigning a puzzled expression, he said, "That's strange as well because you took an interest in it when it was used as a general anaesthetic on your mother in the hospital."

With hardly a moment of hesitation the wily politician said, "Oh, yes. Of course. I'd forgotten what it was called. Obviously, I asked the doctors all about my mother's operation but that's hardly surprising. I'd forgotten the name, that's all." He turned away and sneezed violently.

Haseley Abidh's allergy was the inspiration that Brett had been waiting for. With a smile, he continued, "You said you knew Isabella McShine only by reputation, so you've never been in her home. We wouldn't find your fingerprints there."

"That's right," Haseley said indignantly.

Brett nodded. It was the answer he was hoping for. If Abidh *had* visited Isabella, he was probably convinced that he'd not left a trace. He would have worn gloves and maybe a hat to prevent leaving any hairs. But he was probably unaware of the latest developments in forensic science. Brett glanced at his watch and said, "We don't want to distract you longer than necessary so we can leave it at that. We've got to prepare for tomorrow morning. That's when we've got a forensic team going into Mrs McShine's place to take samples for DNA profiling off any and every surface. Very thorough. You'd be surprised how sensitive the method is. Not just blood. One hair would do it." Brett paused and then, very deliberately, dropped his bombshell. "Or one tiny drop of saliva."

Haseley hesitated, swallowed and then sneezed into his hand. When he looked at his palm, it was covered with a fine spray of spit.

"I've got to hand it to you, man. That was brilliant." Allen laughed aloud. "You looked him straight in the eye, delivered a spinner and trapped him terrific. Tonight, you want me to put officers around Isabella McShine's place to see if Abidh turns up with a bottle of disinfectant and a mop." He chuckled again.

187

Gusts of wind swirled round the corners of the buildings and ballooned the detectives' clothing. It still wasn't cold – not like British wind – but it was becoming too strong to be a welcome relief from the unrelenting sunshine.

Brett replied, "I don't think so. The more people who know about this trap, the more likely word'll get out about it. Remember, Abidh's got some pretty weighty friends. Maybe your boss, so if you make it official…"

"You want us to tackle it ourselves!" Allen cried.

Brett laughed and slapped Allen's shoulder playfully. "It's all right. I know it's Friday. I wouldn't be so cruel as to ask you to join in. We'll do it. Me and Clare. You go and make music."

Clare nodded her approval. "Relax. Enjoy." Then she added, "You can put Umilta McBurnie under surveillance, though. Just in case Abidh consults her first. Especially after Brett's sledgehammer comment about her visitor on Wednesday."

Brett added, "Or in case she has any other male visitors we should know about."

Brett looked piercingly at Allen but the West Indian detective merely nodded and said nonchalantly, "Uh-huh. Sounds sensible to me. I'll get on to it."

At about four o'clock, when Allen declared himself to be off-duty, the trio split up. Just as they were separating, something remarkable happened. The wind blew itself out. Suddenly, stillness was restored and the constant whistle in their ears ceased. Brett looked up, sighed with relief, and said, "Hey, just like that, it's gone. Amazing. Hattie must've passed us by."

Allen shook his head ominously. "No. It's bad news." His expression was grim as he sniffed the air like an apprehensive animal. "Haven't you heard of the calm before the storm, man? This means it's going to hit us. One hundred, maybe one hundred and twenty miles an hour. I'll give you some advice. Tonight, you'll be all right but stay indoors and hold on tight to something."

Brett looked at Clare and smiled. "I'll take that advice. I can think of just the thing." In cracking a joke, he was underestimating the danger. But it would not be long before Brett appreciated and respected the extraordinary ferocity of the Caribbean climate.

Brett and Clare bought a take-away meal from Jemma's Sea View Kitchen, left their car outside the café and walked along the wild forest track to Isabella McShine's shanty. It was just like her daughter's meagre home. Inside, it was like a garden shed. It had none of the luxuries and convenience of houses in Sheffield. There was no electricity and no gas. Isabella had prepared her meals over a wood-burning stove. There was a water supply but Brett doubted its purity. She must have done all her washing by hand in water heated on the stove. For light, she must have used candles. That didn't matter to Brett and Clare. After nightfall they would have to sit in the dark anyway so that they didn't alert Haseley Abidh to their presence, if he showed up and proved his guilt.

On a shelf that ran almost the length of one wall, there was a row of jars containing all sorts of leaves, skins, roots, insects, and unidentifiable specimens. It looked like an outlandish pharmacy.

Brett and Clare squatted on the two battered old armchairs, probably hotel outcasts, and shook their heads in despair. "I'm not sure I could live like this," Clare said quietly. "Even at the age of twenty-six, never mind if I get to ninety-two."

Brett nodded. "You could if you didn't have a choice. You're strong enough. And what did Allen say? Resourceful enough."

"Yeah. I guess so, but I'm also spoilt by a decent salary and a cushy life in England."

As the wind began to rustle and shift the dried banana leaves overhead, Brett replied, "Me too. It's not so much this place I find depressing, though, it's really the gap between the mansions of the rich and the hovels of the poor that gets me. If everyone lived in palaces, I'd be comfortable in one myself. If everyone lived like this, I'd be fine here. It'd be normal and I wouldn't know any different."

Clare agreed. "Yes. By these standards, even you and I are rich."

"Exactly. It makes me feel guilty," Brett admitted.

"I don't think you can blame yourself for life's inequalities. You can blame politics and politicians if you like."

"By the end of tonight, we might be blaming Abidh for quite a lot."

They lapsed into silence. But it wasn't complete. The wind had begun to surge again. The walls of the shack creaked. From every side, draughts pervaded Isabella's home. The strength of the squall was increasing alarmingly. It felt like sitting in a tent during a gale, wondering if the thin protection would still be there in the morning. Both of them were suddenly uneasy and alert.

"Do you remember England's hurricane?" asked Clare. "1987, October, I think."

Brett smiled wryly. "I'd just left my mum and dad in Kent. Moved up to university in Sheffield. They really copped it down south. Nineteen people died. But it was the trees I remember most from the news. All present and correct one afternoon. Thousands flattened the next morning."

"And what speed was that wind?"

"Eighty miles an hour, if I remember rightly. Ninety at most," Brett answered.

"Allen said it gets up to a hundred and twenty here."

"Mmm." Brett said no more.

"And we're in a flimsy hut, surrounded by trees."

Brett put his hand on her arm. "We stay put and hold on tight."

An hour later, they peeked cautiously out of the side window. The evening was unlike any other that they had experienced on Tobago. No longer romantic, it was scary. The clear air had apparently been replaced with fog. But it wasn't actually fog. The wind had become so severe that it had whipped up the waves and carried droplets of seawater along with it. The gale tasted salty. The tuneful cries of birds had been exchanged for the ugly roar of the storm. It made Brett and Clare wonder where all of the birds went. Where did they take shelter? The trunks of the nearby palm trees were all bowed in the same direction. At the top of each trunk, the ball of foliage had been transformed. Now, the blurred fronds looked like the feathers of a head-dress, all forced back by the rushing wind. A plastic bag and an empty can flew past. The bag slapped against a tree trunk, wrapped itself round, and then took off again restlessly.

Quickly, Brett and Clare withdrew, their hair suddenly tangled. Together they strained to close the shutter and keep out the wind. "Wow!"

But the hurricane was as determined as a wild animal to get at them. It sank its claws into the wide leaves above their heads. Half of the roof suddenly peeled back, flapped a few times against the rest of the canopy, then ripped away and disappeared. The hole above them revealed flying debris. Leaves and litter carried on the violent roar of the wind. "This is getting bad," Brett shouted over the racket.

"Allen said we'd be all right." Clare wondered who she was comforting. Her partner or herself.

"Yeah," Brett replied in a sceptical voice. "That's what worries me. He used his gig to get out of this job and drop us right in it."

Clare shook her head. "I still don't think he'd set us up," she cried.

Unbeknown to the troubled British detectives, a male figure had squatted down at the front of the shack where he was sheltered from the worst of the gale and cursed the weather. He steadied himself and used his body to screen a large can from the remaining wind. From his pocket, he extracted a lighter. At the third attempt, he lit the cloth that was pushed loosely into the mouth of the container and soaked with petrol.

Inside, Clare bellowed, "I think we're wasting our time. No one in their right mind would be out on an evening like this."

"Since when has a murderer trying to destroy the evidence of his crime been a perfectly sane and rational being?" Brett responded.

It was at that moment that the door of the hut flew open and a can of petrol with a flaming wick was flung inside.

It landed in the middle of the room and immediately petrol splashed over a large part of the floor. Ignited by the burning material and fanned by the inexhaustible supply of air from the smashed ceiling, the flames bloomed.

Barred from the door and window, Brett and Clare retreated at once into a corner of the shack, as far from the flames as possible. But there was hardly anywhere to go. Their faces searing, they turned their backs on the fire. Clare took a deep breath and slammed her right foot into one of the upright logs that formed the side of the hut. There wasn't any choice. The only way out was through the wooden wall. She had to demolish it. The pole budged but did not collapse. Her second kick felled it, though. She guessed that she had to kick out five more to make enough of a hole to squeeze through. But she doubted that she had time before the flames took the skin off their backs.

As soon as she'd kicked down the second wooden slat, Brett let out a pained cry. His shirt was on fire.

He turned and slammed his back against the wall to put it out. "I'm OK," he yelled. "Carry on!"

But the third log would not yield to Clare's power. Even after three shuddering kicks, it refused to budge. With the fire getting out of control, Brett and Clare were trapped. It separated them from the water supply and from the table and chairs that they could have used to reach the gaping hole in the roof. It was hopeless. The flames began to scorch them.

In a series of small explosions, Isabella McShine's glass specimen jars shattered in the intense heat, scattering glass and their tattered contents into the air. On the other side of the hut, the window shutters were blown away by a furious gust of wind. Then the hurricane that was taunting them also saved them. It brought a sudden wave of torrential rain. The shower pelted down through the damaged ceiling and gushed in from the open window. Almost immediately the spray dowsed the flames.

Instantly drenched by the downpour, Brett and Clare ran out of the shanty into the guts of the storm. A few trees were being bent so much that they dipped down across the track like bowing giants. At least two trees had already collapsed.

Squinting against the wind and rain, they struggled to spot the man who had tried to fire-bomb Isabella's woodland home. "There!" Clare shouted. She pointed through the murk at the outline of a figure down the track. He was heading in the direction of the Sea View Kitchen.

Brett nodded and they both set off. Yet running was useless. And impossible. They had to lean sideways into the wind too much just to stay on course and on their feet. And it was dangerous. With only one foot in contact with the ground, their hold on the earth was too tenuous. The hurricane could have just whisked them away like the plastic bag. Bent low, they staggered onwards. Two steps forward, one enforced step sideways to keep balance. Almost immediately they became breathless. The wind knocked the air out of them and they had to work very hard just to oppose the elements. The deluge came at them almost horizontally and stung their sides like needles. The chase became even more perilous when whole branches hurtled across the track like spears thrown by angry natives.

Nature was out to prove that it was powerful and irresistible. Mere humans could only cling on and watch in awe the destruction of their frail environment as the cylindrical wall of cloud swept across Tobago, wreaking havoc. Out at sea, storm surges formed. The walls of water battered the reefs and slammed into the coastline like tidal waves. Near Scarborough, the storm picked up a small yacht and dumped it unceremoniously on the second green of a golf course against the bare trunk of a dying palm. The boat looked like a sad discarded toy.

Yet in Speyside, Brett was determined. He knew that if the fire had not already decomposed any traces of DNA in Isabella's home, if the rain was not washing the evidence away, then the wind might remove the whole structure. If he could not get close enough to identify the suspect for certain, his clever ploy would fail miserably. The combination of a fire-bomber and a blinding blizzard would beat him.

It also struck Brett that the fleeing man could have had an entirely different motive for the attempted arson. He might have intended to destroy Brett and Clare, not residues of DNA, because they were getting too close to the truth. The thought depressed Brett. He could think of only one person who knew that they were hiding in the hut.

He gritted his teeth and pushed on. Beside him, Clare was just as stubborn. She refused to submit to the storm. Ahead of them, the man was trying for the third time to scramble over a fallen tree trunk. Under normal circumstances a single jump would have sufficed. But now, each time he mounted it, the hurricane shoved him back. Brett and Clare closed in on him. Trying too hard to move quickly, Clare stumbled and sprawled on to the muddy path. Whipped by the wind and jabbed by the rain, she laboured back to her feet and continued the fight. The downpour washed the dirt from her at once. The chase felt like wading through neck-deep water with an overpowering current constantly driving them off course.

In front of them, their quarry finally surmounted the barrier and continued along the path at a rakish angle towards the coast.

"Who is it?" Brett bellowed. "Can you see?"

Clare shook her head. "Black and male, though. But only Abidh knows we're interested in the hut."

Brett could not hear all of her words but he read her lips. "Abidh *and* Allen Rienzi," he yelled.

In the wet, the track became increasingly slippery. Often they could not resist skidding sideways. They made best progress by not lifting their legs at all but by sliding their feet forward as if skating. When a large leaf smacked into Brett's face like a sudden hand slap, he lurched across the path and landed on his left arm. Shocked but unhurt he crouched and then forced himself up into the dreadful squall again. Despite the tumbles, Brett believed that they could make up a lot of time at the fallen tree. As a pair, they could help each other over it. First, Clare scrambled on to the large trunk. So that the wind did not drive her back again, she kept low and Brett supported and pushed her. Really, she rolled over the barricade. Brett used the same technique and, with Clare pulling him, he soon joined her on the other side. Saving their breath, they didn't speak to each other. They worked together as a team by instinct. Not far behind the man who had set fire to the hut, they took off in slow-motion but punishing pursuit. The storm made no distinction. It pounded Brett and Clare as much as it assaulted their target.

Almost instantly, Brett lost his footing again on the treacherous surface. Powerless to regain his balance, he flopped with a curse. Clare glanced back at the untidy heap on the track and decided that he was not likely to be injured. She carried on. But, out of the corner of her eye, she saw something that brought her to an immediate halt. "Brett!" she cried at the top of her voice. "No!"

A second tree began to topple towards him, its roots excavating a large clump of earth.

Even if Brett could have got upright in time, the hurricane would have stopped him escaping from the falling tree. Instead, he decided to take as much cover as possible. He slumped back against the first trunk and nestled to it like a baby to its mother.

The tree crashed down on him.

Clare did not think, she just reacted. The man who had become much more to her than a working partner was buried, probably hurt. She battled back to him. Clinging to the newly fallen obstruction and looking over it, she saw that Brett was trapped between the two trunks. Luckily, the second tree had collapsed across the first so it had not crashed right to the ground and crushed him.

Brett looked up at Clare and groaned. His expression told her that he was in pain but he yelled as loud as his winded lungs could tolerate, "I'm OK. You've got to go after him. Leave me."

"And if this trunk slips off the first one?" she shouted back. "You're dead. Then who's going to deal with Forensics?" Suddenly, eerily, she found herself shouting for no reason. The storm had disappeared. Clare was reminded of being caught bawling into someone's ear at a disco when the music stops. The downpour became a faint drizzle and the wind subsided. The sky was clear as if there had never been a hurricane. Still thinking more of Brett than the suspect, Clare jumped on to the trunk and put her hand down into the gap towards Brett.

Brett should not have accepted her help. He should have repeated his order that she could go after the arsonist who, freed from the storm's grip, was accelerating along the path. Yet Brett clutched her hand gratefully in his. It had never felt so good. He let her heave him out of the hole. His upper body responded but one leg simply refused to move. His numbed left foot was trapped. "It's stuck," he grunted, pointing weakly down towards his ankle.

"Hang on," she said. "I'm coming down."

"No, Clare. Time to get after him. Free me later."

She ignored him. In her mind, she had already justified why Brett came first. It was nothing to do with forensic liaison. She needed him. She couldn't risk his life.

A branch had bitten into his foot at the ankle. Not enough to break the bone but it had probably cut off much of his blood supply. She glanced at her partner and said, "I'm going to yank on the branch that's got you. Drag your leg away when you can." Taking a deep breath, she grasped the gnarled wood that was taut like a spring over Brett's foot. At first, Clare made no impression on it. She shifted to a different position to get a surer grip. She took a deep breath and applied her considerable strength. Even so, the wood was under so much tension that it barely moved. Clare leaned back, using the weight of her shoulders and back as well, until her muscles twitched and strained. Through gritted teeth, she muttered, "Get ready." She put all her remaining energy into one last tug. The branch cut her hands but eventually the wood creaked and moved.

Brett murmured, "That's it! I'm out."

Clare let go straight away. Taking no notice of the toll it had taken on her bloody palms, she said, "OK. Let's get out of here. No more lying down on the job." As she spoke, she climbed back to the top of the trunk and pulled Brett up. "Can you walk?" She leapt down on to the path and put up her arms to help Brett slither carefully to the ground.

He made sure that he set down his right foot first and then tested his left gingerly on the mud. "Can't feel a thing," he said with a nervous smile. He began to hobble along the track. "That's getting a bit better. Some feeling's coming back." There was a cut across his forehead and nasty bruises on both arms. His shirt was ripped and probably hid more wounds. No doubt, his back was burnt and blistered. But he didn't complain. He was very lucky. He had escaped serious injury. He looked at Clare tenderly and nodded in appreciation. "Thanks, Clare. You're pretty good. Let's see if we can pick up his trail."

"You're going to run on that ankle?"

"Kill or cure," Brett replied. "Come on."

With every step Brett winced, but his ankle felt freer. At the end of the track, emerging on to the main road by Jemma's café, which had lost its roof and balcony, he was jogging almost normally. But he was also spent, and racked with aches and pains.

The road was quiet. In the dusk, Brett and Clare could not see anyone. "If he had a car, we've lost him," Clare said, panting for breath. "Gone. But if he came by boat before the storm..." She pointed along the road towards the private jetty.

Together, exhausted, they walked towards it.

When they got there, they saw a launch pulling away from the sheltered wharf. The ocean was still rough but the storm surges had abated. Brett and Clare looked at the second motor boat moored at the small quay and then at each other. They both felt as though they had been pummelled for twelve rounds by a heartless and expert boxer, but they still had a job to do. "Let's go!" they agreed.

"Got any sea-sickness pills on you?" Clare asked as she knelt to undo the ropes.

Staggering about like a drunk in the pitching boat, Brett said, "This business of just being an adviser is a doddle, isn't it?"

Brett was still trying to figure out how to start the motor when a car screeched to a halt back on the road. Its headlights glared and its horn blared. It was Allen Rienzi who jumped out and dashed to the jetty.

Brett sighed with relief. "A sight for sore eyes," he muttered to himself. He was relieved because it was not Allen in the boat. Also, Brett was grateful that he would get some help with the launch. "Am I pleased to see you!" he called out.

Yet Allen was shouting forcefully, "No! Leave it."

"But he's getting away," Brett objected.

Allen gazed into the night sky. "No, he isn't," he said mysteriously.

Abandoning the boat and joining Allen, they asked, "What do you mean?"

"The man's had it. Come on. I'll explain in Jemma's basement."

In the candle-lit cellar, Jemma, her family, and three guests were sheltering. "How are things up there, Allen?" Jemma asked nervously, shuffling everyone along to make room for the newcomers.

Upbeat, Allen said, "It's not too bad." Then he had to admit, "But you've got a new roof to find and a balcony to repair."

"Lord, protect us," she muttered to herself.

"What's happening?" Brett enquired, delicately rubbing the various raw spots that he could reach. "Isn't it over?" He slumped on to the floor and massaged his swollen, bleeding ankle.

"You don't know hurricanes," Allen replied. "And our friend out on the sea thinks we got the edge of the storm – like it said on the news. But we didn't. Hattie turned. We got her full blast. I was on my way to get you but I had to take shelter in a friend's basement. I don't know how you two survived it. It's like a huge doughnut, man. Raging winds round the outside and, in the middle, nothing. The eye of the storm. Absolutely calm. That's where we are now. I used the eye to come and rescue you guys but I saw the launch taking off. I reckoned you'd be crazy enough to be right behind. Any moment, we'll be hit by the opposite side of the hurricane."

Slowly, it dawned on the British detectives that Allen had just saved their lives. They had barely made it through the hurricane on dry land. It would be unthinkable to be caught at sea. He must have driven like a madman to get to them in time.

"Thanks," they murmured in unison.

Allen shrugged. "No problem. Except I had to abandon the gig. Not one could hear the band above the roar of the wind anyway, so it wasn't worth playing." He let out a laugh and said, "Just kidding. Really, we called it off. Everyone was told to stay in ground-floor hotel rooms."

For two more hours they crouched safely in Jemma's crowded but comforting cellar. Thirty minutes of uncanny silence followed by more than an hour of nature venting its anger. Brett and Clare held each other while the hurricane seethed above them and ravaged the island. It sounded like a ferocious war being waged all around. They were both wondering how they had dared to be outside in the first part of the hurricane. They feared that, when they looked back on it, they'd think of themselves as more foolish than brave.

When they emerged from their bunker when the

hurricane had passed, Allen's car was on its side, even more battered than before, leaning against a bank at the edge of the road. Their own car had been crushed by part of Jemma's balcony.

Allen, Brett and Clare pushed Allen's car back on to its wheels. At first, they thought that its engine was too damaged to go but Allen started it at the fourth attempt. Then they cruised back to Scarborough through the bruised island. Allen looked at Brett and said, "You're hurt. I've got a friend who can patch you up."

Brett grinned. "Of course you have."

"Even in the middle of the night?" Clare asked.

"He's no ordinary doctor, not exactly registered," Allen replied with a little chuckle. "But he has good medicine, straight from the rainforest."

"Sonny Bourne?" Brett cried.

"No, man. He's still missing."

"There's something I've been meaning to ask you, Allen," said Brett. "Are there any poisonous spiders on Tobago?"

Allen shook his head. "Nope. But people sometimes get worried about them because they love to hide in shoes."

Brett nodded but did not reply.

At first light, the reckless sailor and fire-raiser was found at Hillsborough Bay, washed up with pieces of wood from his smashed boat. The ocean had disgorged him.

The fruit vendor's van had been no match for the angry gale. The puny vehicle had been tossed and upturned by the storm. It was splintered against the concrete wall of the airport terminal. In the field opposite, near the top of the punctured trunk of a stripped palm tree, a golden-olive woodpecker was drilling a new hole in the dead wood. At Store Bay three of the shacks had been pushed inland by the wind and enormous waves. Gangs of youths were pushing them back into place. A storm was not going to dent the tourist trade for any longer than necessary. Everywhere Brett and Clare looked, men without shirts were boarding up broken windows, fixing damaged bars, restoring electricity supplies and phone lines, retrieving seats, tables and thatched umbrellas from the most unlikely places, salvaging wayward tin roofs, and lifting obstacles from the roads. The younger children were gathering scattered coconuts. When they really wanted to, these people could work right through the heat of any day.

Bad news for the tennis court at Tropikist, though. It had been hit by the wing of a light aircraft. The tarmac was scoured and dented. It would have to be repaired and repainted. The rest of the craft was nuzzling against the side of Crown Point Hotel. It had obviously been lifted from the nearby runway and tossed about like a paper aeroplane.

Most of Tropikist's dining area was bare. Nearly all of the staff were too busy mending to prepare a proper breakfast. Clare and Brett sat together thoughtfully on the grass, surrounded by the debris of the hurricane, sipping fruit juice and biting on big chunks of coconut. It was the only food that the staff could supply. An unsightly bruise had splashed black and blue stains across Brett's forehead. His arms and left foot throbbed remorselessly.

Allen joined them, slouching on the ground. The early morning sunshine had already baked the lawn dry after the rainstorm. He briefed them on the news that the head of the Trade Department had been discovered at Hillsborough Bay. It did not come as a surprise. Haseley Abidh had been taken aback by Brett's suggestion of taking saliva samples from Isabella's lowly property and last night he had fallen straight into the trap.

"Hillsborough," Clare murmured. "That's a coincidence."

"It is?" Allen queried.

"It's a place in Sheffield," she explained. "Where our football team plays."

"An own goal by Abidh," Brett put in.

"What's next?" Allen said. "A trip to Umilta McBurnie, I suppose."

"Agreed," Brett replied eagerly. "It's not all over yet. We need to press her. See if she played any part in the murders. In particular, we need to check if she encouraged Haseley Abidh to murder her husband."

Clare shook her head. "I was all for giving her a bit of stick. But not now. I don't think we should question her as a suspect. Look, I'm here as an adviser and I'd say you could screw this up big time if you're not careful. Go in accusing her of all sorts of things and she'll clam up. We should go to her as the victim's wife and tell her we've cleared it all up. Shut the case. Then sit back and watch what she does." For Allen's benefit she explained Brett's theory about a second lover and then continued, "If she's plotted it all with some other man, she won't be able to resist getting in touch with him and telling him their plan's worked."

Allen inhaled as he considered her opinion. Then he looked at Brett.

Brett nodded. "She's got a point. I'm with Clare on this one."

"Never cross a good woman," Allen said. "OK.

Let's do it like you say."

"And I've got another idea," Clare added. "I know what we should tell her about Abidh. Something that might put her at ease and, if she's guilty, make her more likely to give us the evidence we want."

"Oh?"

"Tell you in the car on the way," she suggested.

"No rush," Allen replied. "Let me get a coffee first. Relax."

"No coffee," Brett remarked. "Power's off."

"Fruit juice, then."

While they finished their makeshift breakfast, Brett asked, "What speed did the wind get up to last night, Allen? Do you know?"

Allen shrugged. "The wind speed recorder got blown away."

Umilta looked beautiful, calm and shocked all at the same time. "Haseley," she murmured as if trying to persuade herself that what she had just heard could possibly be true. "You say Haseley killed Ellis and the McShine woman and now his body has been washed ashore after the storm?"

The three detectives all nodded and watched her closely.

She shook her head and sighed. "Did he really love me so much that he would…? I couldn't love a man who would go to such extremes." She dabbed her eyes with a dainty handkerchief. "But I did."

"Umilta," Clare asked, "there's something you

didn't tell us about that yacht trip on the afternoon Ellis died. Did Haseley stay with you all the time?"

Umilta shifted uncomfortably in her seat. "Well, I didn't like to mention it. You see, I didn't suspect Haseley – not for a moment – so I didn't see the need to tell you before. I thought it was obvious that Jason Lipner had... Anyway, we set off together – a lovely afternoon – but Haseley left me in charge and went off for a good while in the lifeboat. He liked to unwind sometimes by going full tilt in the speed-boat." To Clare, she said, "Men are like that, you know."

Clare did not question her further on the point and merely nodded. "What did he do when you got back to the harbour?"

"He had to go and take care of some business, he said. He was a busy man."

"The business he took care of was Isabella McShine," Brett announced. "He switched one of her concoctions for a poison called ricin. Or he used ricin to lace something she was about to take. A trick he probably learned from Sonny Bourne."

Umilta muttered, "I can barely believe it."

"Sorry," Clare said, rising from her seat. "But that's it. We've closed the case. At least you can get on with your life now, knowing what happened to your husband. It's all over. I'm just sorry we had to tell you it was Haseley Abidh."

Once they were outside and away from the house, Clare said, "That's the next trap laid. Have you got a surveillance expert in there, Allen?"

"The best I've got. With the best photographic equipment. If she gets a visitor, we'll have close-ups within minutes."

The whole island was recuperating. Everything happened slowly. Car journeys were punctuated by the need to shift obstructions from the roads. Phone calls did not happen. A lot of islanders were securing their own lives and homes before they could turn their attention to tourists and work. Eventually, though, word came back from the depleted forensic team that Allen had despatched to Speyside.

"Good news?" Brett enquired hopefully.

Allen shook his head. "They couldn't find any saliva samples. Mainly because they couldn't find the shack." He grinned broadly and said, "It's just as well you were forced out last night – or you might've been in Grenada by now."

Brett sighed. "Well, we've got the next best thing to proof. Haseley Abidh obviously believed the evidence against him *was* there."

It was a quiet midday on Sunday, the sun beating down as if storms on Tobago were unthinkable, when an officer slapped a package of photographs on to Allen Rienzi's desk. His only comment was, "Hot stuff."

Allen spread the stills out on his desk with Brett and Clare peering over his shoulders. There were shots of a white man arriving by launch, coming up the path to Umilta's house, greeting her. Through the windows, there were photos of them talking, kissing, hugging. There was no doubt that the visitor was offering more than sympathy.

"Who is he?" Brett didn't recognize him.

"Would you believe it?" Allen murmured. "American botanist and rainforest guide. Up to no good again."

"The missing Sonny Bourne!"

"Who do we tackle first?" Allen wondered, talking to himself.

"Time for another visit to the hospital," Clare advised.

It was Clare's idea to let Umilta believe that Haseley Abidh was dead. But he wasn't. He had been washed ashore alive, although he had been badly thrashed by the sea.

Standing at the bedside of the mangled politician, Clare asked quietly, "Was it your idea to murder Umilta's husband?"

Haseley nodded but then groaned because it was obviously painful. "Yes. Absolutely." His voice was burdened with regret when he added, "McBurnie wasn't interested in divorce so it was the only way Umilta and I could be together."

"Umilta didn't even hint that she wanted you to do it?"

Abidh had not yet lost his sense of chivalry. "No."

In a way, Clare felt sorry for the man who had

killed two people. He was badly hurt and still he was making a gallant effort to shield his lover. It was probably his love for her that had kept him alive while the storm battered him mercilessly. And now Clare was about to deny him that lifeline. Haseley was about to be devastated.

They had been told by the doctor that they could not tire the patient. They had been restricted to a short visit. Clare had to get it over with. "We've got to leave soon because you need rest. But let me just say this. If I told you I don't believe Umilta's motives for starting an affair with you, you'll assume we're setting another trap. Trying to get you to incriminate her. You need more than my word. I'm going to leave you with some photos. I'm sorry. Take a look at them." She laid the envelope on Haseley's bed. "They were taken this morning. After you've seen them, you'll want to think about Umilta McBurnie and then you might want to change your mind about your solo performance. We'll give you half an hour to think about it."

One of the photographs was still crushed in Haseley's hand when they returned to his bedside. He looked up at them with tears in his eyes. "I should have known when I told her there was a loose end I had to take care of," he muttered. "Sonny Bourne. I told her I had to get rid of him. That would have protected me. There'd be no link between me and ricin and Mrs McShine. You see, I got Bourne to fix up a meeting between Lipner and Mrs McShine. I had to. I couldn't risk Lipner having a real alibi when I was framing him. So I set up one that I could knock down afterwards just by sacrificing the old woman. Then it was Bourne's turn. That would have been the end of the link. But Umilta said no. She only wanted her husband out of the way. She was happy enough for me to kill him – so we could be together – but she didn't want any more deaths." Haseley sneezed and then winced with pain. "She said she'd given way with the McShine woman because she was at the end of her life anyway, but Umilta drew the line at a man in his thirties. I never doubted her. It never occurred to me that she might be having a relationship with him." He closed his eyes for a few seconds. "I asked if she knew Bourne. She said she'd met him a few times when he got together with Ellis to discuss conservation. She thought she could persuade him to make himself scarce till you arrested Lipner and closed the case. She said it was better than another murder."

"You planted the bottle of thiopentone at Xenox?" Brett asked.

"Yes," he said distractedly. He was still thinking of the woman who had tricked and used him. "I was hurt, maybe puzzled, when she wouldn't let me take the last step to protect myself, to distance myself from the murder. I was going to work out a way of making it look like Lipner had killed Sonny Bourne. The final nail in Lipner's coffin. I'd have convinced you, I know. Now it all seems so sordid. I wish I'd never met her!" He wept quietly. "All the while, Umilta was waiting for you to charge Lipner before she ditched me. And if you didn't, she would've exposed me! I wasn't a lover, I was a scapegoat."

"Mr Abidh," Allen chipped in. "I need to be clear about something. Whose idea was it in the first place to kill Ellis McBurnie?"

Haseley sobbed, "Umilta's."

"We've got a problem with all this," Allen said. "She'll just deny it. And so will Sonny. There's no evidence except your word. They'll get away with it because any lawyer will say you're a murderer who's been found out and is trying to share out the blame. She'll play the sweet innocent."

"I know," Haseley murmured. "She's been very clever. Now, I feel so desperate, so ridiculous. Stupid. I loved her and she duped me. I did all her dirty work. I was so dazzled by her, I didn't think about anything but how to be with her. I've been blind and selfish." The broken politician hesitated for a long time and then looked up at Allen. "I'm sorry. I trusted her totally. I don't have any evidence against her. Only my word."

Brett and Clare sighed aloud. They knew that, without a courtroom exhibit, the word of a politician was not enough. With Abidh arrested and the whole story revealed, their task on Tobago was over. But the case was not complete. Umilta and Sonny had got away with it.

It wasn't the outcome they were hoping for but Allen was determined that the two loose ends would not spoil his party at the conclusion of the investigation. The beach was a riot of colour, booze, music, dance and food.

When the band took a break, Allen slapped Clare and Brett on their backs and chimed, "Cheer up. Have a few beers. We got the main man, we took the big hitter's wicket. Confession signed and in the bag. That's worth celebrating."

"But…"

"No buts. We did a good job." He turned and shouted to Lee Teshier, "Lee, as a fisherman, tell these two that reeling in the big fish and letting two slip off the hook's not bad."

"It's not bad!" Lee shouted back merrily.

Behind Lee, a forlorn character lingering unseen in the shadows of the palms strained her ears to hear the rest of the conversation.

"There you are," Allen said. "We can live with a couple of dropped catches. But, believe me, long after you guys have gone back to England, I'll be keeping an eye on Umilta McBurnie and Sonny Bourne. They must be feeling smug. Any mistakes and I'll have them. I really liked Sonny but right now nothing would give me greater pleasure than charging them both with aiding and abetting murder."

"They deserve it for the way they manipulated and used Abidh," Clare replied. "Icy cold."

"And particularly the way they were happy to let poor old Isabella McShine die just so Abidh could blame someone else," Brett said. "That's no way to go."

"No," Allen agreed. He took a deep breath and then uttered, "But you're not going to ruin my party. Two Caribs over here, Janelle! Don't let our English guests dry out." He dashed away to start up the steel band again.

Once Brett and Clare had drunk too much Carib, once they'd danced themselves out, once Brett's left ankle became too sore to take more punishment, they retired to a relatively quiet area of the beach, sat on the soft sand and relished the atmosphere. For a while they didn't speak. They didn't need to. They were both thinking the same thoughts. They were pleased to have played their part in concluding the island's murder case. They were both looking forward to getting back to the comforts of their own homes. And neither of them wanted to leave.

Softly, Clare said, "I shouldn't have given up the chase on Friday. I could've caught Abidh, stopped him getting hurt. Not very professional for a police officer. I wouldn't if we hadn't..."

"I know. And if you'd gone down under a tree, you know I wouldn't have been the professional cop. I wouldn't have left you either."

Clare shook her head. "When John Macfarlane lectures about respect but nothing more between partners, I guess he's got a point." There was disappointment in her voice.

After a few seconds, Brett forced himself to say what he didn't want to admit. "From a work point of view, yes." It hurt him to hear his own words.

Once more the waves were lapping luxuriously at the shoreline. The sea was no longer a vicious and angry force trying to obliterate everything in its path and the tropical breeze cooled pleasantly. The night was clear and the moon shone brightly. Further out from the bay, Buccoo Reef had been badly damaged by the mountainous seas during the hurricane's double strike on Tobago. The *Dendronotus* sea slugs had been virtually wiped out overnight. While the police partied, the Xenox team was busy preparing to move its operation to Grenada.

Hushed, Clare recited, "*The seas are quiet, when the*

winds give o'er; so calm are we, when passions are no more."

"What?"

"Nothing," she said, fingering the bracelet on her wrist. Just an old poem."

"Everything's going to be back to normal when we get home, isn't it?" Brett whispered miserably. "Mundane. We'll be ordinary police partners again."

Quoting Brett, Clare said with a sigh, "Sheffield has its attractions but this is very special. Another world. A world where we're … different."

"We're going to relegate it to a short-lived holiday fling, aren't we?"

With her eyes shut tight, Clare nodded. "The events at Isabella's place taught us both something, I guess." Then she looked into her partner's face. "But I hope we're not going to forget what happened here. Between you and me, I mean."

With a meagre smile, Brett touched her bare leg. "No. I won't forget. And I won't regret it, either."

"Good."

Brightening suddenly, Brett asked, "How about coming back here on holiday some time? Real holiday next time. Fancy it?"

His partner grinned. "There's always Christmas. Do you mind missing Santa?"

"I'll pin a note to the chimney, telling him we're in Tobago."

Sneaking up behind them, Allen exclaimed, "How come you two are talking about leaving so soon?"

"It's a pity, Allen, but we're under orders to fly back to Sheffield as soon as this investigation's complete," Brett explained. "I wish we had a bit more time. Time for ourselves. To wind down."

Allen laughed. "Still rushing!"

"We'd better call the airport in the morning."

"Hey, you taught me how a busy Brit tackles crime and I taught you how to dance, loosen up, how to relax. Don't forget my lessons so soon. Anyway, if you call for a flight in the morning, man, you'll make a fool of me."

"Why's that?"

"Well," Allen announced, "three hours ago, I e-mailed your boss in England. I told him I was confident that, with your help, I'd only need another five days to clear this case up. No problem." He smiled broadly. "Now, take my advice. Relax. Enjoy."

Epilogue

It was a dark night. The electric lights from the house were like beacons. Outside, the woman crept through the wild garden and stood for a moment between the bushes and the palm tree that looked like a giant unfolded fan. In front of her was the secluded garden, two empty plastic chairs under a thatched umbrella, and the back door into the house. It was the sort of home that she could only dream about. From where she stood she could see into the kitchen and, to her right, the front room. Through a gap in the flimsy curtains she could make out two people. A white man and an Asian woman, sitting together, raised their glasses to each other and drank. The man had his arm around the woman's shoulders. They laughed and kissed fervently.

In the garden, the woman turned away in disgust.

She steeled herself and then walked towards the back door. Gingerly, she turned the handle. The door wasn't locked. Her heart beat fast as she slipped noiselessly into the bright kitchen. For a moment, she blinked and glanced around. Such a wonderland! And gadgets she could never afford or know how to use. She might be too poor ever to have possessions like these but she had the knowledge. Her belongings came for free from the rainforest.

She saw the opened bottle of champagne sitting in a bucket of ice. Perfect. To herself, she muttered the white detective's words that she'd overheard on the beach. "Icy cold." There was no sound from the lounge so she took the folded paper from her pocket and unravelled it cautiously to reveal a tiny amount of cream-coloured powder that wouldn't leave a trace.

She was satisfied that Haseley Abidh would rot in jail for his crimes but she could not let the two cold-blooded schemers in the front room get away with it. "Forgive me, Lord," Evelyn murmured, as she carefully tipped the powder from the paper into the bottle.